CIRCUMSTANTIAL

RENEE LEAR

To order additional copies of this book, contact:
Bookwhip
1-855-339-3589
https://www.bookwhip.com

Dedicated to all the men and women incarcerated
for crimes they did not commit.

CHAPTER ONE

Gina

Sitting outside on the patio of their favorite Bistro, Gina and Stephanie laugh and toast to their past times being single together. Stephanie is Gina's best friend and will be her Maid of Honor in her wedding in two days.

Gina comes from a prominent family that owns several businesses. Stephanie has been her best friend since middle school. They attended high school and college together and were always inseparable. Gina loves Stephanie as a family member, not just a friend.

"Well I hope that Steven can keep you satisfied. It's so funny that he thinks you're the 'good girl' out of the two of us and you're the one that never went out without at least a three pack of condoms in your purse when we were in college," laughed Stephanie.

"Yes he will be able to keep me satisfied thank you very much. I'm very happy and proud to be able to walk past that part of the isle without buying an economy pack," replied Gina winking.

As the two women laugh and reminisce Gina's fiancé Steven walks out onto the patio and up to their table. He bends over and kisses Gina on the neck then gives Stephanie a deep look as he walks around behind Gina and sits down beside her.

"What a beautiful view for lunch we have here. How is my bride to be and her Maid of Honor this lovely day?" Steven asked.

"We are doing great actually. I think we have everything lined out for the wedding. The rehearsal dinner is tomorrow night and everyone is all set. How about you babe did you get the issue with the tuxes worked out?" asked Gina.

"Yes, they're having one flown in from another location. They're 'so sorry' that they miscounted and almost shorted us a tux. Fucking idiots," sneered Steven.

"Well at least it's worked out right?" asked Stephanie. "We can't have anyone walking down the isle naked can we?"

"I've got it under control ladies, as always. There will be no nudity until the honeymoon right baby?" Steven kisses Gina on the hand and smiles at her. "So are you ready? Don't let me cut your lunch too short but I do have a meeting in an hour. I'd like to get you to myself for just a few before then. Am I still dropping you off at the condo?"

"Yes I'm ready. We're finished we were just waiting on you," Gina smiles and wipes her mouth with her napkin then gets up as Steven stands and pulls her chair out for her.

Stephanie rises also getting her purse and keeping her eyes on Steven. Gina starts walking toward the door and Steven stands sideways motioning for Stephanie to go before him as a gentleman would. As Stephanie walks in front of Steven he falls in place behind her and reaches down cupping her ass in his hand. She reaches behind her and touches his hand then they pull away from each other as they get through the door and Steven takes Gina's hand as they walk out of the restaurant.

The day of the rehearsal Gina was running all over the place doing last minute errands that were taking much longer than she had anticipated. She had forgotten to get a final cleaning on Steven's ring and was headed towards Stephanie's house to get it while talking to her mother on her car's Bluetooth.

"Yes Mom I just came from the caterer. All of that is fine I'm just heading over to Stephanie's because I am really needing to get Steven's ring cleaned so that it's perfect. I can't believe I forgot. I was supposed to do that last week and ran out of time. I never pulled that task over into my list for the next day. I can't believe I did that."

"Honey just slow down. I know you expect everything to always be perfect but sometimes life just isn't that way. You're doing such a wonderful job with this wedding. I can't believe you wouldn't let me hire a wedding planner to help you out sweetheart. You're really wearing yourself out," replied her mother with concern in her voice.

"I'd hate to have to slap the shit out of a wedding planner mother. I have learned the hard way too many times that if something is this important to me I have to just do it myself. I'll make myself crazy either way, so better to avoid the assault charge if possible."

"Why couldn't Stephanie just drop off the ring at the jeweler for you? You know you only have three hours before the rehearsal dinner starts and I'm guessing you haven't showered or dressed yet?" asked her mother.

"I don't know what the hell she's doing mom. I've been calling her for the last two hours and nothing. My OCD is not happy that I'm having to drive over to her house unannounced and without it being something I had planned to do today, but I have no choice. Knowing her she's probably sleeping," said Gina annoyed.

Gina's mother sighed loudly. "Okay sweetheart just calm down. Please don't be late to the dinner just to get the ring cleaned. I'll take care of it first thing tomorrow morning if we have to."

As Gina pulls onto Stephanie's street she slows down as she approaches the house. She parks on the street in front of the house because Stephanie's car is in the driveway instead of in its one stall garage.

"Thank you so much mom. I'm trying to calm down trust me. Anyway, I'll let you go. She's definitely here because her car is in the driveway. That's strange though because she always pulls into her garage." Putting the car in park Gina stares at the house wondering why Stephanie's car is in the driveway. "I'll call you when I'm headed to the reception okay mom? I love you."

"Love you too sweetheart," replied Gina's mother as she hangs up.

Gina gets out of her car and walks up the driveway past Stephanie's car and up onto her front porch. The front door is shut. Gina knocks on the door. When there's no answer she walks over to the window looking into the front room. She sees the TV on, a tray of eaten snacks on the coffee table and two pair of shoes laying on the floor in front of the couch. Looking closely at the men's shoes, Gina's heart skips a beat. They took like Steven's shoes to her but she tells herself that when she bought them they were not the only pair available.

Gina walks back over to the front door and tries the handle. It's locked. With her face and neck now becoming red and her hands starting to shake she looks towards the side of the house that leads to the back patio.

She walks down the stairs walking around the front porch towards the back of the house. As she turns the corner of the house and approaches the eight foot privacy fence Gina hears laughing coming from what she knows is Stephanie's back patio furniture. Walking up to the back gate Gina stands still listening intently. She positions herself so that she can just see through the wood slats in the fence. As she sees Steven sitting on a lounge chair with Stephanie sitting on top of him, Gina's heart feels as if it has been set on fire inside her chest.

"You better be ready for me when we get back," said Steven as he kisses Stephanie deeply and rubs her ass pulling her closer against him.

"Oh you mean when you get back from your honeymoon?" asked Stephanie slyly.

"Don't give me the jealousy bullshit. You know you're the one getting the best part of this. She's the one that's going to have to get fat having my beautiful babies then spend all of her time making sure they're raised according to whatever the fuck is on her list for that day. Meanwhile, this ass of yours had better stay fit, in tact, and available for me to fuck when I want. I'm not paying your house payment so that you can have some stupid ass up in here. We agreed to this years ago so don't pull the marriage card on me," said Steven as he kissed her breasts making her moan.

"Yes I remember. Something about her money and my pussy being what you want and need in life," said Stephanie as she smiled and taunted him. "I know I'll be the one going on 'business trips' with you while she attends PTA meetings. It's all good baby. I'm all yours. Actually it's pretty fucked up because my therapist says that I'm in love with Gina and that's why I'm fucking you."

Steven laughed and kissed her deeply. "Is that right? And what do you think? I know the two of you have been together. Gina told me all about it. What do you think made me want to get between your sweet legs? She described you perfectly." As Steven reaches his hand down the back of Stephanie's pants she begins to moan.

Gina quickly turns away from the back gate and begins to stumble towards the front yard with her hand over her mouth. She was trying not to vomit, not to scream, and not to die right then and there. As she made her way to her car she felt as if she were in a nightmare that she couldn't wake from. Nausea, fear and hatred were all crashing into her like tidal waves.

Mary

Mary stands in her kitchen over the stove tending to the dinner that she was making. From the kitchen she can see into the living room and the evening news had just started. She looked at the clock and it was 5pm. She knew that her husband George would be leaving his work and heading to her and that he would arrive by 5:30pm.

What this also meant, is that Mary had to have the food ready and on the table by the time that he walked in the door. She knew not to leave anything hot on the stove for him to be able to get his hands on. She never knew what to expect, but she did know to try and be prepared for the worst.

From the living room she heard the news anchor beginning the rundown of the evening's broadcast.

"For our top story this evening, Emma Wallace has been found guilty of the murder of her late husband, Alexander Wallace of Wallace Industries. His cause of death was determined to be a Homicide by Ethylene Glycol poisoning, the primary ingredient in Anti-Freeze. Mrs. Wallace had begun poisoning Mr. Wallace three months before his death after learning of his affair with his secretary. Mrs. Wallace was to inherit 10 million dollars upon the death of Mr. Wallace through an insurance policy. In accordance with their prenuptial agreement, she would gain only 1 million dollars if they were to divorce," stated the anchor.

Mary had been listening so intently to the report that she hadn't turned the pork chops and they were now overly done on one side. Hearing the sizzling she looks down and begins to panic trying to figure out a way to salvage the chops. Turning them over they weren't burnt, they were just more done than she knew George would like. She began to pray that he had a good day at work.

"Oh God, no," she said as her hands began to shake while she tries to get everything finished.

As Mary finished up with the potatoes and green beans and began to get everything ready to be put on plates she heard George's truck coming up the dirt road leading to their trailer. She knew from the time she heard his truck that she had about three minutes until he walked in expecting his food on the table.

Mary, hands shaking, pulled herself together and got the food on the plates putting the darker side of the pork chop down on the side of the mashed potatoes. She put the plates on the table and made herself a glass of lemonade, quickly put it next to her plate, then went to stand next to the door waiting for him to walk in.

"Please Lord be with me. Although I live in the valley of the shadow of death I know that you are with me. I will fear no evil," prayed Mary as she heard him walking up the steps and then opening the door.

As the door opened a dirty rugged George walks in the door slamming it behind him. George shoves a 12 pack of beer into her arms and his lunchbox on top of that then begins taking off his coat and boots while Mary puts the beer in the refrigerator and gets one out then places it on the table in front of his food.

George walked into the kitchen belching and farting, pulled out the chair and plopped himself in it. Mary sits down only after he has sat down. She looked at her plate and waited for George to start eating.

As George began inhaling his food he stopped long enough to turn over the pork chop and notice that it was dark brown on the bottom side.

"What the fuck is this shit?" he spat with food in his mouth.

Mary knew better than to try and give an excuse. She simply looked down and stayed as still as possible trying not to anger him further. She was hoping that he would just keep eating.

"You've been cooking my pork chops for fucking years so how the fuck you still gonna fuck it up? What the fuck were you doin that kept you from paying attention to my fucking meal?" Looking at her with his face twisted in rage he then turned and looked at the TV.

"You watchin that TV again? What the fuck did I tell you about that?" George reached across the table and slapped Mary in the side of her head.

Mary braced herself trying not to fall out of the chair, or to cry, or make a sound.

"Turn it on at 5 so I can fucking have it on when I get here and that's it! And you still can't keep from fucking up." George stood up pushing his chair back and walking towards the TV.

Mary looked at George and began to shake furiously. She knew there was nothing she could do, except brace herself for pain. She began to fade out of her mind and try to go to another place as she watched George take the power cord from the back of the TV and then head straight back to the table for her.

"I'll solve this fucking problem. I'll take this fucking cord with me to work then when I get home I'll give it to you to plug back in. I'm gonna fucking give it to you as a reminder every day," screamed George as he pulled Mary out of her chair by her hair onto the floor and started whipping her with the cord.

Calvin

Calvin stood in the break room using the hot water spout on the coffee machine to fill his cup with water for his Vanilla Chai tea. He was trying to drown out the sound of his co-workers behind him laughing and bragging about their escapades the night before.

"You're a fucking genius bro. I mean my wife loves it that we go out every Wednesday night for our 'racquetball game'. She says that gives her time to do whatever the fuck she wants to do and I'm home by 9. Usually she just watches some stupid ass show that she knows I'd never let her watch if I was home. Stupid reality shit," said Jason smiling and taking a drink of his coffee.

"Mine's been having girl's night with her friends. They go get drinks wherever the newest Happy Hour list is. She fucking loves it too," laughed James holding up his coffee mug as if toasting the moment.

Jason laughs and says, "The fact that we have to shower after the 'racquetball game' is what's truly genius. No worries about her smelling this or that, not having to worry about making an excuse to wash up. Fucking genius bro seriously."

"My problem is that Sara is starting to act like she wants me to see her every Wednesday night. Now what the fuck. I already have a wife. That defeats the fucking purpose of having an affair. I don't need two wives," said James.

"Dude, stop fucking the same girl. Why did you tell her you have every Wednesday night? Stupid ass. You asked for that. Only tell them one night a month that way you can see at least four different females in a month. You're the fucking genius and you're not even doing it right. Get your mind right man," laughed Jason as he slaps James on the shoulder.

Calvin begins steeping his tea bag in his hot water and sighs to drown out the morons behind him. Unfortunately he had sighed loud enough for them to hear.

"What's the problem dipshit?" Jason yelled towards Calvin's back that was still turned. James and Jason both turn toward Calvin to begin taunting him as they often did.

Calvin simply closes his eyes trying to ignore them. He takes a sip of his tea and then takes a deep breath.

"I know you hear me Calvin," said Jason. "Let me guess, you can't turn around because you have a fucking boner from listening to us talk about getting pussy. Am I right?"

As Jason and James laugh and give each other a high five, Calvin slowly turns and looks at them both without any expression at all. He stares at them momentarily and then walks out of the break room and back towards his desk with Jason and James still laughing like idiots behind him.

The next Wednesday Calvin left the building early to be in his car across the street from the company parking lot and ready to follow Jason. He was curious if this Wednesday night event was truly as Jason had described it.

After a few minutes Jason and James come walking out of the building together with smiles on their faces. Calvin is sure they're making reference to their "racquetball game" for the evening. Jason walks away from James laughing and gets in his car.

As Jason pulled out of the parking lot Calvin falls into place about two cars behind him. Calvin knew that Jason was not familiar with his car. Jason always left at least five minutes before anyone else and was never early so he had never actually seen Calvin in his car before.

Jason made his way to the lofts just on the edge of downtown. Calvin's lips pulled to the side in a smile. He knew that he wouldn't have to worry about being noticed on a quiet residential street as he waited for Jason.

Three blocks ahead Jason braked and signaled that he would be parallel parking on the right hand side of the street. Calvin went up a block and a half more, then parked on the left side of the one way street they were on. He watched as Jason got out of his car, grabbed his duffle bag out of the back seat, and then headed up the stairs to the entrance of the building of the lofts he had parked in front of.

Trees lined the street and there were several people walking their dogs and jogging. This seemed to be a very busy area yet as people passed one another they rarely if ever acknowledged each other.

As darkness fell Calvin decided to take a walk around the block to see if he could see into the loft. He walked towards the building and noticed that most of the windows didn't have window treatments. If any they had solid blinds that were either up exposing the window fully or down blacking the window out. He smiled as he looked up and saw Jason plainly through the window. He was on the second floor and although the only light was from the TV it was at least a 52" which lit up the room. He was sitting on the couch kissing a blonde and was pulling her shirt off. Calvin put his hands in his pockets and rounded the block before getting back in his car to wait.

Calvin looked at his watch; it was now 8:33pm. Jason had just emerged from the main building door of the loft freshly showered, duffle bag in hand. He got in his car and pulled out. Calvin fell in behind him once he was a block ahead. Calvin knew he was headed home.

As Jason turned onto a residential street and began to slow down Calvin pulled onto the block behind him then into the driveway of a home with a real estate sign in the yard. He put his car in park and watched Jason pull into driveway of a house further down the block and wait for the garage door to open before pulling in. Calvin looked at his watch and noted that the time was 8:58pm.

Jasmine

Jasmine looked out the window in awe of the view. They were going through a huge wooden gate with decorative iron work leading into the community where her new stepfather Henry's mansion was built. They were driving up the side of a mountain and could see a beautiful view of the ocean to their left. She smiled as she listened to him describe the area.

"The deed restrictions state that each main dwelling must be a minimum of 10,000 square feet so as you can see, each residence is stunning," said Henry as he pointed down the side of the mountain. "Each lot has at least 10 acres so we're not all on top of each other, which of course we love."

"Oh Henry we're going to love it here! It's so beautiful! What do you think Jasmine? Isn't it just breathtaking?" asked Priscilla her mother.

Jasmine smiled trying not to get too excited and said, "Yes it's beautiful. I've never seen anything like this before. Well, maybe on TV or something, but not like this. Is your house as big as those?"

Henry smiled smugly, "I'm the developer of this area. Mine is the biggest."

As they reached the top of the mountain they came to another large gate that was the entrance to the huge circle drive and fountain in front of Henry's mansion. Jasmine gasped at all of the beautiful colors in the landscaping surrounding the property itself. There was too much for her eyes to take in.

After half an hour Henry had taken them through the entire property leaving her suites for last. At the top of a beautiful staircase were a set of double doors. As they walked up to them Henry had a huge smile on his face. Jasmine knew that her rooms were behind these doors and she was trying to contain her excitement.

Opening the doors in a grand gesture Henry began to give them a tour narrating as he went. "And so my lovely Jasmine, as you can see, you have the entire top wing to yourself. This is the main area that you can use to lounge in." Picking up a remote and clicking it towards the wall, it begins to separate revealing a huge flat screen TV.

"Anything you could wish to watch is at your fingertips trust me. And it's a Smart TV so you know you can access the internet and do whatever you need to do. I'm sure you'll need a tutorial on how everything works but once you get it down you'll love it," he continued then motioned for them to follow him through the suite.

"You have your own little kitchenette here in the event that you get hungry. We don't want you having to walk ten minutes to the kitchen from here and your food getting cold in the process. Nothing too fancy, just a microwave, double burner flat plate, toaster oven, and a refrigerator of course." Henry smiled showing her that the refrigerator was already stocked with sports drinks, juice, water, salad, fruits and anything else she could think of.

"Oh honey this is so lovely! We've been sharing a room for so long you won't even know what to do with yourself with all of this space. You'll get lost in your own room now," Priscilla cupped Jasmine's face and kissed her.

Jasmine looked at Priscilla trying to hide her annoyance and smiled.

"And follow me please ladies," said Henry as he motioned them past the kitchen area down the hallway to a beautiful opaque glass door.

Henry opened the door then stood sideways motioning for them to go in. As they entered Jasmine's mouth dropped open. There was a king size wooden four post frame with a wooden canopy that was decorated as if for royalty. The bed was so large that it sat on its own upraised platform. She would have to step up to even get to the bed.

Jasmine walked up and ran her hand across the bedding. She looked up and noticed that the top of the canopy was a mirror. She had never seen a mirror above a bed before and thought it strange but kept a smile on her face.

"What do you think? I can always get you different bedding if you don't like the color or design," said Henry smiling and putting his arm around Priscilla.

"It's wonderful. I love it. Thank you," said Jasmine shyly.

Hours later Jasmine is sitting in the media room yawning as the credits roll on the big screen in front of her. To her right, her mother is passed out with her glass of wine half empty next to her. On the other side of her mother is Henry who is stretching and tucking the blanket around Priscilla.

"Did you like the movie?" Henry asked Jasmine smiling.

"Yes it was great. Even more great that we got to sit here and watch something that's in theatres and not have to worry about the crowd," Jasmine smiled back at him.

Looking at his watch Henry gets up and extends a hand to help Jasmine up.

"Let me walk you to your suite so that you don't get lost," he said as she took his hand and he helped her to her feet.

Walking into her room with Henry right behind her made Jasmine feel uneasy. This was her first night in the mansion and the first time she had been around Henry for more than a few minutes. He had been dating her mother for only a few months when they had suddenly married. She had just come from living in a one bedroom apartment and an unstable living environment, courtesy of her irresponsible mother; to living in a mansion on the top of a mountain in less than three months.

Henry walked in front of her and over to a dresser that matched her bed. He opened a drawer and pulled out a nightgown that was satin with spaghetti straps. He held it up with one strap on each finger and showed it to her.

"Here you are my Jasmine. Just go behind the dressing shade and change into this," he said as he motioned to a folding partition in the corner behind him.

Jasmine didn't know what to do. This didn't feel right but she didn't know if she should be alarmed or not. He was smiling as if all were okay and he was simply being caring. Slowly Jasmine walked towards him, took it from his hands then walked behind the screen to change.

When she emerges Henry is sitting on her bed and has pulled back the covers. He motions for her to come and get in the bed. Jasmine has never been "tucked in" by a man before and feels very awkward. She doesn't even know who her own father is. Reluctantly, she walks towards the bed and climbs into the covers.

Henry smiles at her and strokes her hair. Jasmine says nothing and stays still not knowing how to react.

"So my beautiful Jasmine, I'm told that you will be turning 16 in a few months, is that correct?" he asked.

Jasmine nodded her head and tried to smile.

"Well, I'll be more than happy to buy you whatever car you wish. I'm not sure if your mother has explained our new arrangement fully, but I want to make it clear that this is a package deal. As you can see, when I want something, I get it. This room isn't decorated in pink ponies because you're a young woman, not a little girl. Look up into that mirror," he said as he tilted her chin upwards. "Your body looks like a woman's body, doesn't it."

Jasmine said nothing but felt fear, panic, nausea and hate rush over her. She began to shake but said nothing and tried to have no expression.

"You are going to have everything you've ever wanted Jasmine. Everything," said Henry as he ran his finger across her lips.

The next morning Jasmine did not want to get out of her bed. She had never felt so paralyzed in her life. She wanted to tell her mother what had happened but she didn't know how.

Hearing a car beep from outside Jasmine jumped out of her bed and ran to the window. She could see Henry's Bentley at the gate waiting for it to open so that he could leave. She quickly pulled on her clothes and went to find her mother.

After searching through several rooms Jasmine finally found her lounging outside by the pool with a mimosa. Shaking and wringing her hands together Jasmine approaches her mother scared to tell her what had happened.

"Mom, can I talk to you?" she asked nervously.

"Oh morning my Jazzy. Yes baby what is it?" she asked taking a drink.

Jasmine walked to the lounge chair beside of her mother and sat down slowly. Priscilla patted her leg and pointed towards the view of the ocean. It looked like they lived in a castle that overlooked the sea.

"Isn't it stunning! We made it baby. We finally made it!" Priscilla smiled and took another drink. She looked at Jasmine and noticed that she looked ill. She raised her sunglasses and looked closer at her.

"What's wrong Jazzy? Are you sick?" she asked.

Knowing that she was about to devastate her mother, tears began to stream down Jasmine's face. Priscilla sat up and put her glass on the table then turned to Jasmine grabbing her hand.

"What's wrong? What is it?" she asked wiping the tears from her face.

Jasmine's hand trembled as she put her hair behind her ear and began to tell her what happened, "I ah…..I don't really know how to say this mom," she cried. "Um, last night, Henry walked me to my suite and then he………um……he…put me to bed."

Jasmine jumped as Priscilla's grip on her hand began crushing it. Her face flushed from the pain as she looked at Priscilla who was scowling in her face.

Priscilla jumped up and began pacing back and forth. She took the sunglasses off the top of her head and pointed them at Jasmine screaming, "Don't say another fucking word Jasmine! Not one word."

Jasmine felt like she had been hit by a truck. She was staring at her mother in disbelief as tears streamed down her face.

Priscilla stopped pacing, turned her back to Jasmine, looked at the ocean and screamed. She then turned back to Jasmine and began pacing again.

"I know that you're pissed off that your friends are an hour away and that you're going to have to change schools and I'm sorry about that Jasmine. But this is going too far." Priscilla walked over to Jasmine and pulls her up by her arm then makes her look at the view.

"Look at that!" she yelled as she held Jasmine's chin in place. "Do not fuck this up Jasmine. Your teenage bullshit is not going to win out this time. No fucking way."

Jasmine pulled away from her mother. She had not expected this reaction. She truly thought that her mother would believe her.

"Mom, are you serious?" asked Jasmine wiping her face and taking a step back. "Did you even hear what I said? This isn't about my friends, this is about me." She started to cry again as she spoke, "He touched me mom."

As soon as the words left her mouth Jasmine felt the hot sting from her mother slapping her across the face. As soon as what she had done registered, Priscilla slapped her again, this time splitting Jasmine's lip.

"Now you fucking listen to me. You are almost 16 years old. I have fucking sacrificed for you my entire life. I have spent the last five years selling jewelry to these blood sucking bastards and it's finally my time to be on the other side of the counter. You know good and damn well that you're not a virgin Jasmine. I caught you fucking Tim when you were 13 years old. If we would've stayed in that shit hole you'd probably be pregnant within the year and your entire life would be shit. At least here you have a chance to be around prominent people so that you can be taken care of for the rest of your life. Use your fucking head Jasmine!"

Priscilla takes Jasmine's arm and walks her over to the lounge chair sitting her down. Jasmine is in a state of shock; listening to every word her mother has to say as if each one is another slap. It wasn't that Priscilla didn't believe her; she simply didn't care.

"Now I'm sorry that this is happening to you at such a young age, but at the same time you should be happy that it is. This way as soon as you're 18 you can marry into money and be out of here." Priscilla began to stroke Jasmine's hair. "All I'm asking you for is two years honey. I'm sorry baby but Love is in the same category as the Easter Bunny and Santa Claus. It just doesn't exist. Not really. We do what we do, to get what we can get. That's it, and that's all."

CHAPTER TWO

Gina

Thoughts about Steven and Stephanie's affair were ringing in Gina's ears was so loud that she couldn't make out the words coming from the best man as he gave his toast. Steven was to her right and Stephanie was to her left. She was sitting at the wedding table at her reception looking out at the almost 400 guests that were in attendance.

Gina began looking around the room adding up the cost in her mind again. They had spent over $50,000 on the entire wedding. Everything in her had wanted to call the wedding off, yet she hadn't. She had went through with it, so there she sat, still and dazed between the two people that she loved the most and that she now hated the most.

As the crowd roared over the end of the speech from the best man, Stephanie stood up and tapped her glass to begin her own toast.

"Good evening everyone. I would like to take a moment to toast the beautiful bride and groom as well," she said as she wiped a tear from her cheek. "I have known Gina since we were 12 years old and I've known Steven since he came into her life five years ago. These two people are so dear to my heart. For those of you who don't know, my parents died when I was 15 years old. At that point, Gina's parents were kind enough to take me in and treat me as one of the family. If it weren't for Gina and her loving family, I have no idea where I'd be today."

Gina felt her neck begin to flush as Stephanie's words washed over her. With each word Stephanie had become more emotional and she was now looking directly at Gina and Steven. Steven put his arm around Gina and was looking deeply at Stephanie as she talked. Gina wanted to smash both of their faces, yet she had a show to put on for over 400 people. A smile was the extent of her reaction as Stephanie continued.

"And to Steven. You came into Gina's life and swept her off her feet. I know you'll provide her with the beautiful family that she deserves. I hope that you love and cherish her as I love and cherish her also. I'm so happy that you're part of the family and I truly love you both." Stephanie lifted her glass and toasted the couple as the crowd cheered once more and Gina pushed back waves of nausea.

━━○○○❧◈❧○○○━━

Hours later Gina is ready to head for the hotel. She is winding her way through the crowd greeting and thanking people as she makes her way to the main building. She hasn't been able to find Steven or Stephanie for the last fifteen minutes. The last place they could be is in the kitchen hall. It's the last place she has looked because the food was prepared, served, and would be cleaned by the kitchen staff of the facility.

As Gina walked into the kitchen area she could hear giggling coming from the service area. She knew exactly who it was. Slowly she walked towards the open door listening intently. She could hear Stephanie breathing loudly attempting to quiet her moans. Gina felt as she had felt on the other side of the fence just a few days earlier. She had been trying to tell herself that she had misheard or perhaps misjudged the situation. Surely this wasn't happening.

Stepping into the doorway Gina was looking at a large kitchen island covered in trays with plated desserts that were half or mostly eaten. Steven and Stephanie were standing on the opposite side of the island, side by side facing the doorway. Steven had his left hand gripping the side of the island and his right hand was behind Stephanie. He was looking into Stephanie's face watching the pleasure that continued to spread across it. Stephanie was gripping the island and leaning over it slightly, her face looked as though she was ready to climax.

Gina stood unnoticed for a few seconds, which to her seemed like an eternity. Stephanie finally opened her eyes and jumped the moment she saw Gina standing in the doorway watching them. Steven quickly pulled away from Stephanie putting his right hand in his pocket.

"Okay well you just take all of the dessert you want! I'll keep looking for someone to wrap it up," said Steven as he stepped away from Stephanie and towards Gina. He stopped long enough to kiss Gina on the forehead before walking past her saying, "Hurry up baby we need to be getting in the limo to leave in the next five minutes."

Gina looked at Stephanie wanting to pick up the serving knife that was on the island and bury it in her face. Stephanie recovered smooth as silk and fell right into acting as though she was simply there to snag an extra piece of cheesecake.

"Can you fucking believe how amazing these desserts are? I mean now I understand why you had the meltdown about almost not getting the caterer you wanted. They are to die for!" she said as she scrambled around the kitchen not looking at Gina.

"Yes they are," said Gina feeling her blood turn to ice and her flesh to stone.

Mary

Mary sat down at her kitchen table as slowly as she could. Her body is still hurt from the beating she had endured days before. After getting the bills in a neat stack in front of her she reached up and touched the bald spot on the side of her head where George had pulled out a fistful of her hair. She had a black eye, split lips, and bruising on her arms, wrists, and legs from being grabbed, restrained and whipped with the cord.

The second envelope Mary came to read "Open Immediately" on the envelope. She took a breath hoping that she hadn't missed a payment on anything but sure that she hadn't at the same time.

Unfolding the letter inside revealed a Renewal Notice for the life insurance policy that George had taken out on her. According to this letter he could increase the policy by $100,000 for an extra $25 a month. As she held the notice in her hand, her mind began to wander. She looked past the notice to the newspaper that was sitting on the table.

Mary ran her finger across the words on the front of the paper. *"Emma Wallace is set to be sentenced next Tuesday. She was found guilty of murdering her husband Alexander Wallace by Ethylene Glycol poisoning."*

Mary looked up from the paper and stared out the window to the shed in the back. She looked at the clock and it read 3:35pm. Shaking, she stood up from the table and slowly walked to the front screen door. She looked out the door towards the main road looking for a sign of dust in the air from an oncoming vehicle or any other sign that George may be home early.

Slowly Mary opened the door and crept out of the trailer towards the shed. The door to the shed was open and hanging by only one hinge. Mary walked through the door over to the corner where there were several bottles of oil thrown in a pile. Sitting next to that pile, was also a few Anti-Freeze containers.

She stood staring at them for what seemed like an eternity before finally getting the courage to walk towards them. As Mary reached the container that was flipped over showing the contents and the closest to her, she bent down and stared at the label, but didn't touch anything. She searched the label for the ingredients. She looked at the list and there it was, staring right back at her as if winking at her – 'Ethylene Glycol'.

⸻ ∘∘∘⧓∘∘∘ ⸻

Later that evening as Mary finished doing the dishes she looked at the stack of mail and then over at George in his recliner watching TV. She dried her hands and said a prayer under her breath. She took the stack of bills off of the shelf and then took a beer out of the refrigerator. She walked over to George and handed them all to him. After he took everything out of her hands she went to the couch and sat down staring at the TV in silence.

"What the fuck is this?" asked George as he looked over the renewal for the insurance policy. He held it up to Mary for her to explain.

"It's time to renew the insurance policy you have for me. It's telling you that if you want to spend an extra $25 a month then you can get $100,000 more if I die," Mary answered.

"So how much is that all together then if I do it?" he asked interested.

"The payment would be $45 a month and you would get $150,000 if I die," she said quietly.

"Well hell fucking yeah! For an extra $25 bucks I can get that much money. Damn woman you're worth a hell of a lot more dead than you are alive. Get me the checkbook," he barked at her with a twisted smile on his face.

Mary got up from the couch and with her back to him, pulled the checkbook out of the drawer that it was kept in. She felt her heart flutter with the possibility that she could be free of him. She couldn't let him see that this was what she wanted him to do. As she turned to hand him the checkbook she avoided his eyes and tried to look as forlorn and empty as always. She quickly turned and went back to sit at her place on the couch.

"$150,000. Damn that's a lot of fuckin money. Never thought your sorry fuckin ass would be worth anything, much less $150,000 dollars! The way you fucking mope around here you'll be dead in the next year or so and I can buy myself a maid that knows how to suck my dick right," George laughed as he grabbed himself and then downed his beer.

Calvin

On a Wednesday two weeks later Calvin again sits outside their office waiting for Jason to emerge and take off for his weekly strange. Last week had been the same as the week before. Calvin had to admit to himself that he originally thought that Jason was simply picking up prostitutes and that he didn't have it in him to have non-paying extra marital affairs. Calvin now knows not to underestimate the number of women that will spread their legs willingly for a married man that's attractive and is addicted to attention and ass. Truly pathetic.

Jason came bounding out of the building with James right on his heels once again. The two talked for a few seconds then headed in opposite directions to where they had parked. Calvin started his car and fell into traffic three cars behind Jason after he left the parking lot.

After a few blocks Calvin knew that they were not going to either location they had been to before. This time Jason went deeper into downtown. The streets and sidewalks became congested as Calvin kept a close eye on Jason's car. He was on the other side of the light in front of him but with this traffic he wouldn't get far.

After three blocks Jason puts on his signal then pulls into the valet entrance to Rellington Manor. One of the oldest and most prestigious downtown luxury hotels. Calvin shook his head and grinned slightly. He knew that he shouldn't be surprised at the brazen way Jason spreads himself around every week but he was a bit shocked.

Passing the valet Calvin noted that the time was 5:10pm. He put on his signal and began trying to get over so that he could head back in the direction of Jason's house.

Calvin had been sitting half a block down from Jason's house waiting for darkness to fall. He had watched Jason's wife get home at 6:30pm. She had pulled into the garage then had walked down the drive to check the mail, then had returned to the house shutting the garage door behind her.

Looking around to be sure that no one was watching him, Calvin got out of his car and walked in the opposite direction of Jason's house to go around the block and enter through the backyard.

As he walked down the alley he counted backwards until he knew he was behind Jason's house. They had a privacy fence in the back but Calvin could see through the wood panels. The backyard held patio furniture and a grill. Seeing no dog or anything to be alarmed by, Calvin lifted the latch and walked through the back gate to the back of the house.

Calvin looked through the back door and turned the handle. It was not locked and he could have easily went inside. Instead, he let go of the handle and began looking through every window to get a layout of the house and see how the windows latched. Looking into the kitchen window to the counter he noticed an oversized set of expensive knives.

Calvin turned and went down the back stairs and around the side of the house. Looking through the side window to the living room he could see Jason's wife sitting in an oversized chair with a blanket and a cup of tea watching a movie. Calvin stared at her wondering why a woman like that would be married to someone like Jason. He wondered if she had any idea what kind of a piece of shit she was married to. He assumed that she didn't. For a slight moment he felt pity for her.

After circling around and parking in another location on Jason's block; Calvin looks at the time. It's now 8:50pm and he expected Jason any time. He felt satisfied with the realization that Jason was no doubt, shallow and predictable. Calvin loved playing games. This definitely could have been more challenging, but the outcome would have been the same regardless so he was willing to overlook it. You're only as good as your opponent and with Jason as an opponent, there was no chance of ever making it to the deep end.

At 9:02pm Jason's car rounded the corner in front of him, pulled into his driveway then into the garage shutting it behind him. Calvin smiled, started his car then drove home anticipating the next Wednesday.

Jasmine

A week before her 18th birthday, Jasmine stands in Henry's study staring at the gun case before her. She was wearing two years of abuse heavily. Her bright eyes that were once cheerful and full of life were now empty and hollow.

Jasmine is wearing her long black gloves that go with the black ball gown Henry had gotten her last year for a charity event they had attended. She turned to Henry's desk and retrieved the key for the case where he keeps it hidden.

Turning back to the case Jasmine opened it slowly and began her search again. She ran her fingers across the .45 caliber weapons knowing that they would do the most damage. She wanted to pick up a .45 and begin releasing her anger but she knew she needed to stay calm. She knew she needed to think straight and think clearly.

Towards the bottom of the display case is the pink handled .380 that Henry had bought for her mother. Priscilla had shot it only a few times with Henry. He had made her learn how to use it but Priscilla was more interested in spending money than anything else so it had sat in the case undisturbed for almost two years.

Jasmine had been thinking about this for a very long time. Counting down the months, then weeks, then days; and now it was time. She reached in the case and retrieved the pink .380 of her mother's. Not only did this case display the weapon, each place had additional holders for at least two clips per weapon. Looking at the clip for the gun Jasmine smiled. It was loaded. She knew that was a pet peeve of Henry's because it weakened the springs, but he should've known that her mother wouldn't give a shit and checked it himself. Very thankful that this solved the only problem she had lingering, her mother's prints on the bullets, she closed the door to the gun case, locked it back, and returned the key to its hiding place. Problem solved.

Back in her room Jasmine sat down at her desk and pulled out the drawer containing her stationary. Removing the stationary she wanted to use and placing it on the top of her desk she then put the gun and the clip in the drawer and shut it. She removed her gloves and placed them in her lap.

Looking through her pens in the holder on her desk, she retrieved her favorite and held it between her fingers, rolling it back and forth while her mind went over the words she was to write one last time. Jasmine stared out the window at the birds flying towards the ocean and admired their freedom. Freedom that she would soon have.

Letting out a deep sigh Jasmine leaned forward and began to write the letter to her mother.

"Dearest Mom......I have been wanting to tell you this for almost two years now. I have kept my silence to this point because I know that you love Henry and I know that you love this lifestyle that he has provided for us. I'm telling you now because you've always told me to 'use my head'. I need you now more than ever and I hope you hear me because I'm crying out for you............"

CHAPTER THREE

Gina

Gina heard the sound of the waves crashing on the rocks below her window. She opened her eyes and inhaled deeply taking in the fresh air. They were on their honeymoon in Hawaii and had rented a small condo on the edge of a cliff for the week.

Looking out the window Gina smiled without being able to help herself. It was undeniably beautiful. She then turned to the left to see that side of the bed empty. Seeing the empty space snapped her back to reality and the smile was quickly replaced with despair.

Gina looked around the room for Steven. He was nowhere in sight. Not wanting to find him but feeling compelled to; she gets out of bed and begins going through the cabin in search of Steven.

As she came to the small bathroom off of the main living space she could hear Steven's voice coming from the other side of the closed door.

"I don't know why you're so upset baby. You've known this would be happening for over a year now. You promised me that you wouldn't do this," he said with concern in his voice.

Gina felt her body singe as if on fire as his words fell over her ears and burned her to the core. She was so furious that she could only stand there, still as a statue and let the words wash over her paralyzing her further. A tear ran down her cheek as she continued to listen to him.

"I know baby, I love you too. You just need to calm down and remember the plan. The prenuptial agreement says that we have to be married at least five years before I can get any part of the family business upon divorce. With my position right next to her father, that gives me five years to show him what I can do, which is make him a shit ton of money. Once he knows how valuable I am to his bank account he won't even blink when Gina tells him she wants to divorce me. I have everything under control. You just need to calm down and quit being so fucking jealous. You know I love you Stephanie," he said as he continued to comfort the sobbing Stephanie on the other end.

As his words washed over her Gina felt everything that made her alive drain from her body. She felt as though she had just died, yet she was still standing in the middle of the nightmare. She suddenly felt completely empty. Completely done. She stood up taller, wiped the tears from her cheeks, then calmly turned around and walked back into the bedroom.

Gina pulled the journal she always kept with her out of her suitcase then sat in the chair next to the window and began to write, making sure to first put the date and time at the top of the page.

Fifteen minutes later Gina was sitting in a lounge chair by the window wrapping up her journal entry when Steven walked into the room with two cups of coffee and a smile on his face.

"Morning beautiful!" he said as he put the coffee down on the stand next to her, kissed her on the forehead then walked to the window and started talking as if he was all set to begin their honeymoon.

"So I really wanted you to see the sunrise on the ocean but I couldn't wake you up. Did you get enough rest? Remember the trail that wraps around the cliff with the best view is 4 miles one way so that's 8 miles we're going to cover today. Are you pumped or what?" he asked turning to look at her.

Gina didn't acknowledge him but simply closed her journal, walked to the nightstand to put it back, then turned to get dressed for the walk along the cliffs.

Steven watched her every move and wondered if she had heard him on the phone with Stephanie, yet he didn't care all the same. They were married now and had just spent $50,000 on the wedding. He knew that he could do what he wanted and then some.

"Fucking moody bitch," he smirked under his breath as she went into the bathroom shutting the door behind her.

•••◦❧◦•••

Gina walked behind Steven on the trail that wound around the top of the cliff. There was at least a 500 foot drop to the rocks and ocean below. Although the view was beautiful, the crash of the waves on the rocks was angry. The more she listened to it, the more she became one with the sound of the crashing below them. She felt as though her entire life was crashing in on her, relentless, again and again and again, with no mercy, no pause, as one crash faded another began; just as the waves beat relentlessly on the rocks below.

Coming to an overlook on the trail Steven checked their distance. "This is the 2 mile point. Let's stop here and rehydrate," he said pulling two bottles of water out of the hikers pack he was wearing.

There were several large boulders that appeared to be sitting areas for the overlook. They walked over and sat down taking a drink of their waters.

"Can you fucking believe this view?" asked Steven with a huge smile on his face.

Gina looked out past him thinking that it was the best view she had ever seen and would ever see. When she didn't look at him or acknowledge him, Steven became pissed off and gets up to start a fight with her. Gina didn't like to argue. She was more prone to keeping all of her emotions inside of her. Being out of control was not something she let happen.

"Okay what the fuck Gina?" yelled Steven stomping around the overlook annoyed by her behavior. When she remained still and continued staring out at the view he continued. "So what's the fucking problem Gina? We haven't had a fucking conversation since a few days before the wedding. I thought maybe you were getting cold feet but fuck me, we're married already! Why am I getting the silent treatment and why are you ruining one of the best trips and experiences of our lives?"

Gina sat there listening to him. He wanted to know why. So did she. She took a few more moments to look at the view before taking a deep breath then getting to her feet and facing him.

"Why don't you tell me why," she said. She didn't have it in her to have a huge emotional knock down drag out. She just wanted to know why so that maybe she could find some peace.

Steven stared at her with the usual innocent look. He was the best liar she had ever seen. Five years together and he was fucking her best friend for years, right in front of her face. She wondered if she ever would have found out if she wouldn't have needed his ring cleaned.

"How the fuck am I supposed to know why? Did you forget your fucking list or something? I just thought you've been overwhelmed with the wedding, but we're here baby, look at the view! It's our honeymoon!" He walked over to Gina and put his arms around her and started rubbing her ass. "Why don't you calm down and let me bend you over that rock and relax you a little bit?"

"Tell me about Stephanie," she said with no emotion in her voice. She has had plenty of time for emotions. She had nothing left. Even with his arms around her she kept her arms down at her side not wanting to touch him ever again.

"What about her?" he asked as he pulled back trying to look Gina in the face to get a read on her.

"At what point did you decide to start fucking her? Or, better yet, at what point did you start to love her?" she asked looking into his eyes with dark coldness twisting inside her.

Steven smirked in her face and took his arms from around her then began pacing back and forth letting off steam. "I don't know what the fuck you're talking about. What did she tell you?"

"You know exactly what I'm talking about. Otherwise, there would be nothing to tell," she answered coldly.

"Are you seriously going to pull this shit right now, here? What the fuck Gina? There's nothing to fucking tell I'm just sayin!" he yelled raising his arms as if she was upset he bought the wrong kind of water. He seemed completely unfazed at the severity of the situation.

"You would stand here and talk to me as if I'm not twice as smart as you are. I will say that I just recently found out what you've been doing, so cheers to you. Well done. How many years did you lie to my face and kiss me with the same lips you were kissing her with, fuck me after fucking her?" she asked.

Steven's face went from playing stupid to twisting in a sarcastic grin. "Oh so you're smarter than me? Okay Gina, keep thinking that. If you're so fucking smart why don't you tell me where we go from here? Let me guess, you're going to call Daddy and tell him that I've been cheating on you? This would be the same Daddy that took me to his yacht club and paid for five of us to have escorts for the day. Or the same Daddy that fucks his business partners wife? You can't fucking tell me that you don't see that your Daddy will fuck anything that comes in his direction. He's my mentor. Go ahead and fucking call him. I just followed in his footsteps. Marry the trophy wife to breed with and fuck who I can fuck. Your mom has to know what he's been doing for the past 30 years. She's just smart enough to shut the fuck up and enjoy life. If you're so fucking smart then why are you even confused about the situation?"

As his words beat her down further than she thought possible she simply walked past him towards the edge of the cliff. As she came to the edge she looked down at the rocks below and let the sound of the crashing waves fill her emptiness.

"And how the fuck can you blame me for Stephanie? You're the one that can't go anywhere without her. She was putting her tits and ass in my fucking face from day one. And what did you do when I mentioned it to you? You fucking describe licking her pussy yourself in college and all that shit! What did you expect me to do? In the beginning I thought you were setting it up so we could have threesomes and I'd be down with it," he yelled at her back frustrated at her ignorance.

Gina turned around and put her back to the cliff. She looked down at her feet and the loose ground beneath her. She knew that if Steven were to push her off the edge of the cliff the marks on the ground made by her foot would be a heal mark that kicked the dirt towards Steven and away from the edge. She looked behind her once again at the rocks below, then back towards Steven. She then dug her heal into the ground then swung her leg up as if she had been pushed backwards off balance.

"What the fuck are you doing? Quit messing around Gina," Steven took a step towards her concerned that she was about to try and kill herself. He didn't fully understand what she was doing.

"This time last week I was high on life. I had everything I wanted. A fiancé that I was madly in love with, a best friend that was like a sister, and a father that I adored. Now, thanks to you, I have nothing," she said feeling as if she was being filled with concrete. The weight of the situation was now fully upon her and it was heavier than she could have ever imagined.

"Gina, what the fuck! Just walk towards me, this is bullshit. You know that I love you, your father loves you, fuck Stephanie definitely loves you. Quit fucking around and let's just talk about this," he began to sound desperate as Gina held her arms out to her sides.

"This is how life works Gina. Your bullshit fantasies are just that. In the real world this is how it is. Every fucking show you watch is some scandalous bullshit. Then you have the fucking nerve to stand in front of me and act as if you're fucking Mother Theresa. Come on Gina, you know we can make this work. You may not like the reality of the situation but it is what it is," he said taking a step towards her with his hand out for her to take.

"That's not a reality I'm prepared to live in," she said as she let herself fall backwards and heard him scream her name from the cliff above her as the sound of the crashing waves rushed towards her and she stared at the sky above.

Mary

Mary stood in the kitchen with her lemonade glass in her hand. She looked at herself in the reflection of the microwave and even in that dull image she could see the black eye had continued to spread that George had given her the night before. She lightly touched her cheek and felt the heat still coming off of it.

It had been a month since the incident with the TV cord. She had just finished healing from that. Over the years she had noticed that if George couldn't see a wound visible on her at all times he would make one. She made it a point to avoid the actual mirror in the bathroom.

She looked down at her lemonade glass and then slowly let her eyes move to the window where she could see the shed. She stared at it intently and began to shake. She had never done anything she wasn't supposed to. She had never cared enough for herself to speak out or try to change anything. Looking at the shed, she felt as if it was a portal to another life. All she had to do was get the courage to walk through the door.

Mary looked at the clock which showed 11:37am. She then walked to the front door and again looked out the dirt road to be certain that no one was coming. After standing at the door for what seemed like an eternity, Mary slowly opened it and made her way to the shed.

As Mary walked into the shed she looked over to the pile of empty oil and anti-freeze containers. To the right of that was an old wooden bench that he kept funnels, quarts of oil that were full, and a container of anti-freeze that was half full. Nothing in the shed was clean in any way. Dust, dirt, oil, and trash littered the place and surrounded it as well. All along the floor by the bench were dirty rags. More than she could count.

Mary walked over to the bench and bent down picking up one of the dirty rags. She then sat her glass on the bench and looked at the anti-freeze container. As she stared at it she remembered the report on the TV and in the newspaper. She knew that little amounts over a period of time were the best way to poison someone without wanting to be detected. She also knew that the person being poisoned would end up in agonizing pain as time progressed.

She thought about the pain she was already in and had been in for decades then she slowly wrapped the rag around the lid of the container removing it and placing it on the bench. She then wrapped the rag around the handle and lifted it, putting just a splash in her lemonade glass. She then put the lid back on and placed the container and the rag back exactly as she had found it.

Mary headed back towards the trailer with her hands trembling. As she looked down the main dirt road making sure no one was coming she became overly paranoid that someone had seen her. They lived miles from anyone else so she knew she was imagining things, but the weight of doing something she shouldn't made her feel as if the whole world were watching. Her hands shook so badly that she was afraid the lemonade would spill out. As she climbed the stairs to the trailer and the door shut behind her, she had never felt so relieved.

She went into the kitchen and sat down at her place at the table and began to calm her breathing. She looked out the window at the shed, then back to her glass. She was shocked that the anti-freeze really hadn't changed the color of her lemonade. It still looked like lemonade. As she stared at the liquid her courage began to build. She had endured plenty of pain in her life. Surely, this pain would be worth it.

Slowly Mary raised the glass to her lips and took a drink. As the liquid hit her taste buds then slid down her throat she smiled slightly. It was sweet. She expected it to taste like cleaner or liquor. It just tasted like she had made extra sweet lemonade. Mary tried to contain her excitement as the thought of freedom welled up inside of her.

A weakened Mary made her way to the shed as she had every other day for the last two weeks. She had kept with the same routine. Going to the shed every other day, at the same time, and giving herself the same amount. She knew she had to be careful. If she didn't have the strength to keep up with her chores then George would beat her down and she may not be able to finish. Her black eye was half healed but he had just split her lip open again. Not only was she becoming physically weak, she was becoming mentally weak. She had begun to have times when she couldn't think straight.

A little more than a month after the first time she had walked into the shed, Mary walked up to the bench once more. She was so weak that she could barely move. Once again she put a splash of anti-freeze in her glass. Using the rag she put the lid back on the container, placed it back how she had found it, then dropped the rag behind the table where it blended in with the rest of the filth.

That afternoon Mary sat at the table watching the clock. Her breathing was labored. It had been very difficult to drink the lemonade she had made herself earlier in the day. She looked at the clock and it read 4:45pm. It was time for her to start dinner.

This was the first day that she didn't know if she had the strength to get through everything she needed to do. Slowly Mary got to her feet and went to the refrigerator to start getting what she needed to cook. She looked back to the table at her glass and felt the need to make sure it had something in it, just in case today was the day. After filling her glass half full Mary swirled around the liquid knowing that traces of the anti-freeze were still in the glass.

Mary was so off balance that she could barely stand to finish the meal. She looked at the clock again. It read 5:16pm. She knew that George would be coming home any minute. She wiped the sweat from her face and tried to catch her breath. She had begun to see stars and knew that she would be losing consciousness soon. She just had to hold on a little longer.

As Mary put the food on the plates then placed them on the table she heard the sound of George's truck roaring up the road towards the trailer. This was the first day that she welcomed the sound.

As it grew closer Mary let herself go and began to cough, choke, then she vomited blood on herself. Feeling the room begin to spin she grabbed onto her glass and held on for dear life. As she fell to the ground she made sure to keep the glass in her hands. Mary always drank out of the same glass. She knew that fact would make this easier on the police. All she needed were George's fingerprints on the glass.

George stomped up the porch growling under his breath with his beer bottles clinking. He threw open the door and began yelling for Mary since she was to always be standing right at the door to take his beer and lunchbox. Mary didn't answer but laid still on the floor slipping in and out of consciousness.

"Mary, get your fucking ass in here!" he yelled not seeing her lying on the kitchen floor.

Without Mary there to take his things he wasn't about to bend over and put them down before taking off his boots so he kept his boots on thinking that Mary could scrub the floor for not being where she should be. As he walked around his chair and had a clear view of the kitchen floor he saw Mary lying in the middle of the floor with her lemonade glass in her hand, smelling like vomit. George walked up to her and kicked her in her back.

"What the fuck are you doing? It's not time to take a fucking nap. Get the fuck up," he said as he kicked her again. When Mary didn't move he became frustrated. He threw his beer on the table then bent down and grabbed the glass from her hands slamming it on the table. He then took a handful of her hair and tried to get her to her feet. Mary was completely unresponsive and limp. As George let her body fall back to the floor he paced back and forth pissed off.

"You stupid fucking bitch! I worked all fucking day to come home to have to deal with this bullshit," George screamed at the back of Mary's head.

His attention turned to the table where the plates are sitting with hot food on them. George stepped over Mary's body, sat down at the table, took a beer out of the carton then started eating.

The faint sound of beeping began to get louder; Mary could hear it and was trying to open her eyes. Her body felt like it was made of glass and she hurt all over. When she was finally able to open them she was staring at the ceiling of a hospital room. She was suddenly afraid because she could feel tubes down her throat and her hands were restrained. As she began to try to cough she could hear a nurse calling for the doctor.

"Mary, hello Mary, can you hear me?" asked the nurse who was now standing over her. "I know you're disoriented Mary. Please don't be afraid. You were not able to breath on your own so we've placed you on a ventilator. You're hands are only restrained so that you don't pull the tube out. I've called for the doctor. He's going to look at you and we'll see if we can take you off of this okay? Just please calm down. You're safe here," she said smiling.

As the words washed over Mary a tear fell from her eyes. She closed them and let herself slip back to sleep.

Hours later Mary opened her eyes and focused on a man in a suit jacket and jeans with a badge on his belt, and a cowboy hat in his hand. He had been staring out her window. She reached up and felt her lips taking in a deep breath, happy that the tubes were now out of her throat. As she began to get her bearings the Marshall walked up to her smiling.

"Hello Mary. I'm Marshall Simmons. I don't want to put any extra stress on you but I really need to ask you some questions," he said with concern is his voice.

"I'll go let the doctor know that she's awake," said the nurse as she finished checking the monitor and headed out of the room.

"Mary, I know that you're aware that you're in a hospital, but do you know why you're here?" he asked.

Mary said a prayer in her mind as she looked at the Marshall. For over a month she had played this scene over and over in her head. She knew what she needed to do. She knew that her life depended on it.

"No," answered Mary barely able to get the word out.

"The doctor is on his way in and he can explain your condition in more detail. Mary, what I'm about to tell you may be a shock, so I first want to tell you that I'm sorry." As he spoke he walked closer to her bed and took out a small notepad and pen so that he could makes notes from her statement.

"Sorry about what?" she asked having to clear her throat to speak.

"I'm sorry to have to tell you that you're in the hospital because you've been poisoned," he said looking at her to study her expression.

Mary looked at him confused and repeated his words, "Poisoned? I don't understand. How?"

"Your blood tests revealed that you have a high level of Ethylene Glycol in your system," he said.

"I…..I don't even know how to say that. I don't know what that is I'm sorry," she said as she began coughing.

"Ethylene Glycol is the main ingredient in anti-freeze," he said.

"I still don't understand," Mary replied having a hard time talking.

"Mary, your husband George was the one who brought you into the Emergency Room. How long have you been married to George?" he asked.

"Since I was 17 years old," she said quietly.

"And how old are you now?" he asked.

"I'm 46," she answered.

"When he brought you in he didn't bring a purse or a wallet or any kind of identification for you. Do you know where your purse is Mary?" he asked.

"I don't have one" she replied dryly.

"A woman without a purse is like a fish out of water, am I right?" he asked smiling at her. "If it's not here then where would it be Mary?"

"I don't have one," she repeated with shame in her voice.

"You mean to tell me that you don't own a purse?" he asked confused.

"Yes," she answered.

The Marshall took a moment to look at Mary closer. It had been obvious that she had been abused physically, but he was now starting to get a picture of her mental abuse as well.

"So, where do you keep your driver's license?" he asked.

"I don't have one," she said.

"You don't have one? Do you drive?" he asked.

"No," she said as her voice began to quiver.

"Okay Mary, let's talk about George for a minute," he said hoping that he would get more than a few words at a time from her. "If you've been married to him for almost 30 years you should be able to tell me everything about him right?"

Mary stared at him and a tear ran down her cheek. To hear the number of years out loud from him was like hearing the number of years that she had been in prison.

"Mary, do you love George?" he asked watching her begin to cry. "Does he love you?"

After a few moments Mary looked at the Marshall and answered, "No."

"How long has it been since you had love for each other," he asked.

"Never," was her response as she looked out the window.

"All right Mary. If you've been married for this long and never loved one another, then tell me what has changed in the last few months," he said hoping to find something to go on.

"Nothing. He goes to work, comes home, eats, sleeps, and does the same the next day," she answered.

"And you? What do you do Mary? Do you work?" he asked.

"No. I stay home," she said softly.

Marshall Simmons paused for a moment. He knew that she had most likely not had an actual conversation in a very long time. He also knew that due to the poisoning she wouldn't be able to think clearly, so this was going to take some work on his part to help her retrace her memories.

"Okay Mary listen. Again, I'm sorry to have to put you through this, but, you did not get poisoned by accident. Who have you been around in the last month that would be able to tamper with your drinks?" he asked.

"George is the only person I see," she said quietly.

"That's it? Do you ever leave your property Mary?" he asked.

Mary took a deep breath trying to get her strength to continue, "He drives me to the grocery store once a week on Saturday for 30 minutes. That's all."

"So you're telling me that the only time you leave your property is to go to the grocery store and that you only have a 30 minute window to be at the store?" he asked.

"Yes," she replied nodding.

"Do you have any friends at the grocery store? Do you have any family or friends Mary?"

"No. No one," she replied looking down at her hands.

With shock growing Marshall Simmons looked at Mary knowing that she was the most abused person he had every come in contact with in his lifetime, and that he didn't even know the half of it. He couldn't wait to get a hold of George.

"Mary, when was the last time that you had contact with anyone aside from George? Anyone from your family or from a friend?"

Tears began to run down her cheeks as the years of solitude started to unload from her. She truly couldn't remember the last time she had a conversation with someone that cared for her. This stranger was showing her more compassion than her husband had in decades. She was overwhelmed with emotion.

"I don't know," she answered as she began to cry.

The Marshall grabbed a box of tissues and pulled one out. He gave it to her but she was so weak she could barely raise her hand to her face. He took the tissue from her and wiped her tears.

"Mary, I need you to help me so that I can help you. Has George been around your drinks? Tell me what your routine is like at home, please," he said needing to get her to say what he needed to make the arrest.

Mary tried to gather herself together so that she could recite her story. "I ah…..I always just drink lemonade. I guess he could get to it if he wanted while I was busy cleaning."

"Lemonade?" he asked.

"Yes. That's all I drink really. Or maybe water. I have a glass that I use every day," she said.

"What does the glass look like Mary?" he asked writing in his notepad.

"It's just a glass but it has little yellow flowers on it. They're scratched and faded. We only have a few glasses anyway. It's the only one with flowers," she said.

"Tell me if you've noticed anything different lately," he said looking at her closely.

"Well…..I had been thinking that sometimes it was sweeter than normal. I always put the same amount of sugar when I make it so I did think that was strange. But, I've never tasted anything that tasted like poison," she said looking up at him.

"This type of poison tastes sweet when you drink it," he said. He hesitated before he asked the next question. "Mary, I'm sorry to have to say it like this, but it seems like George had it made. He was able to use and abuse you for decades without anyone knowing or saying anything different. Why would he choose to poison you now? What's in it for him Mary? What would be more beneficial than having someone be, pardon the word Mary, but his slave?" he asked.

Mary took a moment before answering. She needed to appear to be searching her mind, trying to connect the dots. When she knew she should have it, she looked at him and answered, "About a month ago we got a renewal in the mail for my insurance policy."

"And did he renew it?" he asked.

"Yes. He chose the option to pay $25 more in a month so that he can get an extra $100,000 if I die," she said quietly.

"And you're positive that he chose to increase the policy?" he asked.

She nodded, "Yes. I handed him the checkbook and watched him write the check. He put it in an envelope and I put it out for the mailman the same day he looked at it."

"Did you notice your lemonade being sweeter before or after he increased the policy?" he asked writing in his notepad.

"After," she replied letting her life of despair wash over her so that she may have some sort of a look like a woman who had just learned that her husband was trying to kill her. But, since she felt that he had been trying to kill her for years, all she needed to do was look natural.

After the detective wrote a few more lines in his notepad, he closed it then stared at Mary with compassion and concern.

"Mary, when the doctor comes in he's going to explain to you that in addition to you being poisoned you also have broken ribs. The yellow bruising under your eye indicates that in the last month you had severe damage to that area of your face. The lasting elements of a black eye I'm assuming. It took them an hour to document every laceration and scar that you have that appears to be from physical abuse," he said staring at her.

Mary looked away from him and stared out the window. She didn't even know how many scars she had. She had quit counting years ago.

"I need you to tell me how you got your injuries Mary," he said not certain how she would react.

Mary said nothing. The thought of George finding out what she had done washed over her and as fear set in she began to shake.

Noticing her growing fear Marshall Simmons put his hand on hers. "Mary, I know that you're scared. I know that you've been living in hell. All you have to do is tell me who did this to you, and you'll never have to see him again."

Mary looked at him wanting, hoping, and praying for him to save her from her life with George. "What will happen to him if I tell you?" she asked.

"With the fact that he's the only one that has had access to your fluids, along with your statement that he has been physically abusing you, I have more than enough for a warrant for your residence. I'm assuming that I'll find your glass, which will contain traces of Ethylene Glycol, and that we'll be able to find the source of it on your property. But, we have to move fast. I'll be honest with you Mary, when George was questioned about your physical injuries he left. We have not been in contact with him since. We need a search warrant to go onto your property and handle this before he destroys the evidence," he said leaning forward needing her to trust him.

"If he……if he knows that I said anything…….. he'll kill me," she said starting to cry again.

"Mary, he's already tried to kill you. Help me keep him from ever doing this to you again," he said.

Mary looked at him and nodded her head that she would give him a full statement. She struggled to push her fear behind her and began praying that she was about to be free.

Calvin

Calvin sat at his cubicle on Wednesday at 3:00 p.m. and watched as Jason and James walked towards the conference room together laughing and giving each other a high five. The schedule stated that they would be attending a "Safety Meeting" but everyone in the office knew it was a Fantasy Football meeting for the jocks in the office. All and only of whom, were on the Safety Committee. As the door to the conference room shuts behind them Calvin gets up from his chair and heads to the parking lot.

That morning Calvin had waited for Jason to pull in, park, then enter the building. Calvin had pulled up and parked behind Jason's car, backing in towards it. As Calvin walked into the parking lot towards the two cars that afternoon he scanned the area making sure that no one was around and that no one was watching from the windows.

Calvin casually walked up to his own car, popped the trunk, reached inside and grabbed a slim jim, walked a few paces to the back door of Jason's car, quickly pops the lock, opens the door with his sleeves covering his fingertips, grabs Jason's gym bag from his back seat with a covered hand, then locked the door back and closed it. In seconds he had thrown the bag in his trunk along with the slim jim and shut it. He casually headed back into the building looking around and feeling confident that no one had seen him.

The time was now 4:40 p.m., Calvin sat in his cubicle finishing up his last report and listening to Jason and James in the cubicles behind him. They were shutting down their computers and getting ready to go.

"So who's on the menu for this evening?" asked James looking over the cubicle wall at Jason.

"Laurie is on the menu bro," Jason answered licking his lips.

"Is that the downtown hotel chick?" asked James standing up and pushing his chair in.

"No dude she's the downtown loft chick. Let me tell you what, when I bend her over her couch and fuck the shit out of her I have the baddest view of downtown you can imagine. Just the fucking view gives me a hard on," bragged Jason as he pushed in his chair as well and headed towards the front of the office with James at his side.

Calvin smiled slightly. On this particular Wednesday, he wanted to be sure that Jason was seen leaving the building before him. He had originally thought that he would have to go to several locations to try and verify which female Jason would end up spending the evening with, but he had saved Calvin the trouble by bragging about his plans.

At 6:20 p.m. Calvin drives past the downtown loft and sees that Jason's car is in fact parked on the left side of the street. He looked up and could see the flicker of the TV in the window. He didn't feel the need to have to get out so he drove past and circled back around to go towards Jason's house.

At 6:50 p.m. Calvin drove past Jason's house and saw his wife in the window walking around the living room while on the phone. He wondered what she was saying and who she was talking to.

At 8:15 p.m. Calvin got out of his car that was parked five blocks from Jason's house, grabbed Jason's gym bag with gloves on his hands and then started walking back to Jason's.

8:25 p.m., Calvin stops at a dumpster that is four down from Jason's house. With gloves on his hands Calvin took his mask out of his back pocket and pulled it over his head and face. He opened the gym bag and began pulling Jason's clothing out of the bag. He was happy that it was fall and there were a pair of long sweat pants and a hoodie in the bag. He put Jason's clothes on top of his own so that none of his skin cells would be present on any of Jason's things. He pulled Jason's gym shoes out of the bag and put them on as well. He placed his own shoes and the bag behind the dumpster then headed towards Jason's house.

Coming to the back gate Calvin looks through the fence, then seeing nothing quickly entered into the backyard. He walked up to the back of the house smooth as silk, as if he was supposed to be there. Not seeing Jason's wife anywhere in the kitchen or dining room through the back door or windows, he went around the side of the house.

He again looked through the window leading into the living room. Once again, Jason's wife was sitting in her oversized chair with the lights out, drinking tea and watching TV. Calvin checked his watch and it was now 8:30 p.m. He quickly turned and walked towards the backyard then up onto the back porch.

Calvin pulled the strings on the hoodie tighter so that it would cover most of his mask and catch most of the blood splatter. He looked through the glass on the door to the knife set on the counter.

Moving as swiftly as a cat Calvin turned the knob and opened the backdoor that was unlocked. He entered the kitchen then quietly shut the door behind him. He walked over to the knife set and pulled out the 8 in. carving knife then turned and walked towards the living room.

Calvin seemed to glide through the room. He came up behind Jason's wife and held the knife above her for a moment. She sat still watching the TV and giggled before taking a final drink, unaware of Calvin.

In an instant Calvin brought the knife down hard, burying it into her chest. Her tea cup went flying out of her hand as Calvin began raining down blows from the knife. She had fallen to the floor and moved no more than a foot. He had come at her too fast and had sealed her fate with the first blow.

After Calvin counted 27 strikes he stood up and looked around. Blood spatter was everywhere. He smiled under his mask and quickly turned and walked to the rug the dining room table was sitting on and wiped the bottom of his feet so that he wouldn't leave a complete trail down the alley. He then headed for the kitchen. He turned on the water and washed the knife off making a clumsy job of it so that traces of blood would remain. With a wet glove he then put it back in its holder still wet and swiftly left through the back door and headed down the alley to the dumpster.

Reaching the dumpster Calvin quickly stripped off the hoodie and sweats and shoved them back in the gym bag. He then took Jason's shoes off, shoved them in the bag then zipped it and threw it in the dumpster. He pulled his gloves off, then his mask, putting the gloves in the mask and turned it inside out so that everything with blood would be on the inside. He then shoved those into the side cargo pocket of his pants. He pulled his shoes out from behind the dumpster and put them on. He made sure to stay on the pavement so that he wouldn't leave any shoe impressions then quickly turned and jogged off in the direction of his car noting that his watch said 8:35 p.m.

At 9:05 p.m. Calvin sat in his car two houses down from Jason's watching him pull into his driveway and open the garage door. Calvin's upper lip twisted slightly in delight with anticipation of what he knew Jason was about to see.

Calvin started his car and rolled down the passenger side window. He slowly put his car in drive and began to roll down the street towards Jason's house. As he began to pass it he saw the living room light come on and he could hear Jason screaming his wife's name, "LeAnn!" from inside the house.

Calvin smiled wide then rolled up the window and continued down the street for his own apartment.

Jasmine

Jasmine stood in the doorway of the master suite watching her mother sit in her bed in her usual alcohol and narcotic induced state. She looked half awake, yet half asleep. Jasmine stared at the left hand side of the bed which was empty, knowing that in a few hours Henry would be lying there sleeping like a Scotch soaked rock.

Priscilla always slept on the right hand side of the bed since she was left handed and needed the night stand easily acceptable to her left hand. On it was a clock that read 11:08pm, two mostly empty bottles of wine, a small tray of remnants of cheese, crackers, and olives, half empty wine glass, and two pill bottles. Without having to look at the labels Jasmine knew they were Xanex and Ambien.

Jasmine walked over to her mother's side of the bed and sat down beside of her. Priscilla opened her eyes and began mumbling something, still half dreaming.

"Mom," said Jasmine shaking her arm gently.

Priscilla opened her eyes and attempted to sit up grabbing the remote and a book that were in her lap and steadying them. "What is it Jasmine? What time is it?" she asked looking at the clock then grabbing her forehead making it apparent she wasn't happy Jasmine was there.

"It's just past 11. I was just coming to make sure that you're okay," said Jasmine.

"Yes, I'm fine. Why wouldn't I be okay?" she asked in an annoyed sluggish voice.

"You told me that you've been having trouble sleeping lately," said Jasmine keeping her voice quiet and calm trying to soothe her mother.

Sighing loudly Priscilla takes her hand from her forehead and looks at Jasmine. "Yes, that's true. I don't know what's wrong with me."

"Have you taken your Ambien yet?" asked Jasmine. Her entire purpose for the visit was to be sure Priscilla had a heavy dose of it in her system and to get one for herself. Priscilla was extremely predictable.

Noticing that her wine glass was still half full Priscilla reached over and grabbed the glass taking a drink. "No sweetheart I haven't. Can you please hand it to me?" she asked pointing to her pill bottle.

"One or two?" asked Jasmine already knowing the answer.

"I need two baby. Two and a half really would be perfect. If I can just fall asleep then maybe I can stay asleep," she said holding out her hand for the pills.

Jasmine opened the pill bottle then broke one of the pills in half. She handed Priscilla 2 and a half pills and watched her wash them down with the rest of the wine in her glass. Priscilla then pointed to one of the bottles on the nightstand motioning for Jasmine to give her a refill.

"Thank you. Now take one for yourself Jasmine. I'm meeting friends for shopping and cocktails tomorrow so I need to be rested. Please go crawl up with a movie, take your pill, and I'll see you tomorrow," said Priscilla as she laid back and closed her eyes motioning for Jasmine to go.

Jasmine's eyes were smiling but she kept a somber look on her face as she quietly took one of the Ambien for herself then put the pill bottle back on the nightstand and left the room.

Jasmine sat on her bed listening for the front gate. At 12:39am. she heard the gate begin to open and knew that Henry was about to drive through it, then make his way up to her room. After his car pulled through the gate and into its garage Jasmine began to open her window then climbed out onto the roof. Two of her windows stood out from the roof in an arch making the side of it a perfect place to hide.

Jasmine settled down beside the arch and pulled her toes back so that if he were to look out the window he would not be able to see her unless he was hanging half out and specifically turned and looked for her. So far, Henry had never been smart enough to do so, and all she needed was one more night in her hiding place.

Only a few minutes had passed when Jasmine heard Henry enter her bedroom and begin yelling for her. She listened to him look through her bathroom, closets, under her bed, all while having heavy feet. She knew he was drunk and she knew what would happen if he found her.

After cursing under his breath for not being able to find her, Jasmine heard the door to her bedroom slam shut. She let herself relax but stayed where she was. She knew she needed at least another half hour on the roof just to be sure he didn't come back looking for her. She looked up to the moon and takes in a deep breath enjoying the view.

Jasmine sat in her bed watching the clock turn to 2:30am. She had been waiting for this for a very long time. Getting out of bed she walked over to her desk and opened the drawer. She looked down at her black formal gloves that were neatly folded on top of the gun. She slid the gloves on then took the gun, clip, and letter she had written to her mother out of the drawer, placed them on the desk and closed it.

She walked over to her closet, pulled off her nightgown and let it hit the floor. She reached in the closet getting out her black hoodie then grabbed her black leggings and pulled them on as well. She pulled the hood up onto her head and looked in the mirror at her reflection. The only part of her skin that was exposed was her bare feet and her face. She had taken plenty of ballet lessons and was prepared to literally be on her toes if necessary. There would be no footprints left behind.

Jasmine walked back to her desk then put the clip in the gun, chambered it, picked up the letter and headed out of her room.

As Jasmine walked through the master suite towards the bedroom she could hear Henry's snores overtop of the 24 hour newscast that was playing loudly on the TV. Reaching the doorway she looked in to see her mother still in her upright position but clearly sound asleep. Henry was predictably on his side of the bed on his right side facing the bathroom, away from Priscilla and from the doorway. Jasmine didn't need to see his face to know that he was definitely out. Jasmine paused looking at them both. She had already done this over and over in her head thousands of times. She thought she would have been more nervous than she actually was.

Calmly Jasmine walked over to her mother's side of the bed thinking that Priscilla being left handed made this almost too easy. Jasmine unfolded the letter she had written her mother and placed it in her lap. She then took her mother's left hand and placed the gun in it. Priscilla didn't stir, she simply stayed limp in her self-induced coma as Jasmine slowly pushed her body on its side towards Henry, holding her hand with the gun and bringing it up towards Henry's head.

When Priscilla was on her side Jasmine used her body to shield herself against the blowback from his blood, wrapped her left hand tighter around her mother's putting her trigger finger on top of Priscilla's. With only one eye visible above her mother's shoulder and her arm shielded behind Priscilla's, Jasmine aimed the gun at the back of Henry's snoring head and very easily applied pressure to her mother's finger which pulled the trigger.

As soon as Jasmine felt the shot she let go of the gun and knelt down on the side of the bed. Her ears were ringing loudly and the room began to spin for just a moment. She blinked then began to focus and looked at the floor. She smiled satisfied that there was no blood spatter from Henry on the carpet to have to worry about stepping in. That made her a little happier that she had stuck with the .380 mm rather than the .45 she originally longed for.

Jasmine put her left hand in the front pocket of the hoodie then got to her feet and watched as Priscilla tried to shake off the heavy curtain of pills and alcohol to figure out what had just happened. Jasmine began walking backwards towards the door as she watched Priscilla look at the blood that was all over her. She dropped the gun in her lap on top of the letter that was now covered in blood as well.

"What is this?" Priscilla said softly as if trying to figure out if she were awake or asleep.

"You finally cared about your daughter enough to kill that sick fuck. That's what this is," said Jasmine calmly from the doorway. Jasmine took the hood off of her head keeping her left hand in her pocket. Luckily, that was the only part of her that had blood on it.

Priscilla looked at Jasmine with disgust and hatred and wiped her cheek. As she looked at her fingers she started to shake. She turned and looked at the hole that was now in the back of Henry's head, and at the blood that was flowing freely from it into the bed beside of her.

"What the fuck is this!" she screamed beginning to panic.

Jasmine simply stood still in the doorway staring at her. As she recounted the last two years of waking nightmares, she felt no pity for her mother at all whatsoever; instead she felt Priscilla was getting off easy.

Priscilla began trying to get the blood off of her hands and face and had started to cry. As she began to come out of her fog she looked closer at Jasmine and what she was wearing.

"What did you do Jasmine? Why are you dressed like that?" she asked still trying to figure out exactly what was happening.

Jasmine stared at her before saying anything. For a brief moment she remembered being in the park with her mother when she was 4 years old, when a smile from her mother could make everything sad go away. Staring at Priscilla now covered in blood, reminded Jasmine that was a very long time ago, and that mother had been gone for years.

"I didn't do anything. This was all you," said Jasmine softly.

"Jasmine stop fucking around! What did you do!" screamed Priscilla becoming more enraged and frightened as the realization that she wasn't dreaming began to fully set in.

"I came in at 11 o'clock and gave you that letter explaining what a sick twisted bastard Henry is. We cried; you told me that you would take care of it; you gave me an Ambien and sent me to bed. That's all I know," said Jasmine enjoying the panic wash over Priscilla as she looked at the gun in her lap, the blood on her hands, the letter in her lap, and then to the hole in Henry's head.

"No, no, no, no, no, this can't be happening," said Priscilla shaking her head back and forth, "it can't be."

"It is actually. The good news is that you can say that you snapped and lost it after you read the letter and that you didn't plan on this happening. With my letter to back up that story then you should just get 10 years instead of life in prison," said Jasmine with a slight smile on her face. She couldn't wait to see how this was going to play out. Either way would be a win for her.

"You little fucking bitch! What the fuck have you done? I didn't shoot him! I couldn't have. You did this. You hated him!" screamed Priscilla crying and shaking.

"That's absolutely true, I did hate him," said Jasmine smiling. "So happy to say that in the past tense now. Extremely fucking gratifying actually."

"I'm going to tell the police that you did this Jasmine! How fucking could you!" Priscilla screamed crying.

"Sure good luck with that," said Jasmine calmly. "You're sitting in your bed with a letter from me telling you that your husband would rather be in my bed than yours; he's lying next to you with a hole in his head made from your gun that has your prints on it, loaded with bullets that also have your fingerprints on them. And, when they do a GSR test on you, which stands for Gun Shot Residue, they'll find it on your left hand and arm, because you did in fact pull the trigger."

Jasmine watched as Priscilla started to break down further knowing that what Jasmine had said was true. Priscilla began crying not for the lack of her being a good mother, or from her losing her husband, it was simply because her 15,000 square foot lifestyle had just started to crash around her. She looked around the room as if trying to absorb all of the materialistic things she loved so much.

"Of course you can always go with your story; I dressed up, snuck into your room, and did all of this because I hated Henry so much.

Which keep in mind that if you do go with that story, then you're going to have to explain why I hated him so much. And to do that, you're going to have to admit that when I told you about that sick fuck two years ago, you chose to ignore me and let him have his way with me like I was a fucking toy. Before you can even dial 911 I'll have hidden these clothes somewhere and I promise you they'll never be found. All the evidence will point to you, as it already does, you'll just look like the cold hearted bitch that you actually are."

As hatred took hold of Priscilla she looked at Jasmine then picked up the gun and pointed it at her. "And what if I just kill you Jasmine, then what?"

Jasmine had fully expected Priscilla to turn the gun on her. Self-preservation was the only thing her mother knew. She looked deep into Priscilla's eyes before answering. "Then you get to wear orange for two lifetimes. Sounds like a great plan to me. I'm sure the females at a maximum security prison will love to have you to play with. And as far as I go, you killed me the day we moved in here."

Priscilla lowered the gun and began to cry. "I can't go to prison Jasmine, you know I can't," she said wrapping herself in self-pity trying to look for a way out of the situation.

Jasmine watched her cry for a few moments before answering, "Then there's only one thing left for you to do."

As Jasmine's words hit her ears Priscilla began to quiet her crying and steady her breathing. She wiped the tears from her eyes, cleared her throat, and straightened out her hair. Once it appeared that she had come to terms with the only option that didn't end up with her in a cell, she looked up at Jasmine one last time.

"Just tell me why Jasmine. You're going to be 18 in less than a week. He was going to pay for you to go to college anywhere, give you anything. Why did you have to do this?" she asked truly not understanding the depth of the pain she had caused Jasmine for allowing her to be abused.

Thinking back to the first day that Jasmine had told her mother what Henry had done, she could recall every word that Priscilla had said to her and exactly the way she had said it.

"I believe you said I needed to 'use my head'. Wasn't that it? That I need to learn to 'do what I can do, to get what I can get', wasn't that right?" she asked coldly. "This is me, listening to you."

Priscilla's face turned to stone. She sat up taller in the bed, straightened out her nightgown and hair once more, then picked up the gun and looked at Jasmine with complete and utter emptiness in her eyes.

"Good bye Jasmine," she said as she put the gun to her left temple then pulled the trigger.

As the shot rang out Jasmine did not take her eyes away even for a second. She watched as her mother's brain blew out the right side of her temple covering the wall, the bed, and Henry's lifeless body beside her. A small smile played at the corner of Jasmine's lips. She knew Priscilla would never allow herself to be arrested. She knew it.

After several minutes taking in every detail of the room, Jasmine turned and headed towards her bedroom to take her pill then go to sleep. She knew that the maid would be there at 9am. It was just a matter of how long it would take her to get to the master bedroom. Jasmine knew she would be awakened by either the maid or the police shortly after nine to tell her what had happened during the night while she slept.

CHAPTER FOUR

Gina

Steven sat at the table of the condo looking distraught waiting on the police to arrive. He had waited almost an hour before calling the police after Gina had went over the cliff. He couldn't decide what to say. If he said she purposely fell then he would have to explain why. If he said she accidentally fell then it would just look like a freak accident and he would have to play the grieving widower. When he called he just said that she had fallen off the cliff. He had been trying to figure out exactly what to say when they got there and repeated it over and over in his mind so that his story wouldn't change. He had decided not to call any family until after he had spoken with the police so that he could concentrate. He knows he absolutely must have a solid story before contacting any of them.

After what seemed like an eternity he heard a knock at the door and went to open it. There were two detectives standing at the door with a few uniformed officers in the yard waiting.

"Good morning. I'm Detective Makani, this is Detective Alamea. Are you Steven?" he asked.

Steven could only nod his head yes and let them in. He walked back over to the table and sat down. The two detectives had come inside behind him while the officers stayed outside. Detective Makani pulled out a chair and sat down across from Steven while Detective Alamea slowly made his way around the condo.

"I'm sorry for your loss Steven," said Detective Makani as he took out a pad to take notes on.

"Thank you," said Steven still numb to the situation.

"You said that your wife's name is Gina, correct?" he asked.

Steven nodded his head yes.

"I would like you to start by telling me why you're here and how this morning started," he asked Steven trying to read him for a sign of anything but a grieving newlywed.

Clearing his throat before beginning Steven stared at the top of the table as he spoke, "This is the first day of our honeymoon. I got up before her and went to watch the sunrise. After I came back in I made coffee for us then took it to her in the room. After that we got dressed and took off for the hike. We wanted to get in the full 8 miles and have time to shower and dress for dinner."

"You say she was awake when you went into the bedroom with the coffee?" asked Detective Makani.

"Yes," he answered.

"What was she doing? Was she still in bed?" asked the detective.

"No she was up reading or something," said Steven. He had remembered that when he walked back in the room with the coffee he had expected her to be asleep but she had been up with a book in her lap he thought. At the time he hadn't cared what she was doing so he hadn't taken the time to actually pay attention.

"What was she reading?" asked Detective Makani.

"I don't know. She was always reading or writing. Always had something in her hand, kept a spiral in her purse, constantly making lists. I couldn't keep up," said Steven truthfully.

Detective Alamea was making his way into the bedroom of the condo. To this point he hadn't found anything out of place or strange. He scanned the room looking for alcohol, pills, drugs, signs of a struggle, anything. It was obvious that they had either just gotten there or were just leaving because most of their things were still in their suitcases. This wasn't the type of place to rent for an evening and it had plenty of closet and dresser space. He knew people that rented these cabins weren't the kind of people to have their clothes wrinkled in a suitcase for an extended period of time.

Seeing nothing in the main area he walked into the bathroom. Toiletries were out for both of them. Everything looked normal. He began opening the drawers and cabinets again looking for pills or drugs. Finding nothing he sighed and exited the bathroom back to the main area of the bedroom.

He then walked over to the first nightstand and opened the drawer. Inside was a phone book, pens, stationary and some delivery brochures. Closing that drawer he walked to the nightstand on the opposite side of the bed. Opening it revealed a journal neatly placed in the center of the drawer with a pen placed perfectly beside it.

Detective Alamea stared at the journal and smiled. Over the years it had been his experience that finding the journal of an "accident" victim is always a good thing. He picked up the journal and flipped to the last entry which was dated for that morning. As he began to read his smile faded, turned to a deep frown, then he looked over his shoulder at the door behind him towards the room Steven was in.

"So what time do you think you started out on the hike?" Detective Makani asked Steven.

"I don't know exactly. I know we reached the two mile point about 9 a.m. That's where we stopped for a drink and that's where she….." Steven couldn't help but be shaken up. He still couldn't believe she had done that. Just hours earlier he had a beautiful bride and a great life in front of him. He hadn't seen this coming.

"Steven I know this won't be easy but you're going to have to walk us up to the point where she fell," he said knowing that there was only a slim chance that they would recover her body. The longer it took to get to her, the less likely they would be to find her.

Detective Alamea enters the room from the hallway looking at Detective Makani squarely, "Are we ready to take a walk?" he asked nodding at his partner to let him know that he had found what he was looking for.

Detective Makani read his partners signal clearly. They had worked together for over 10 years and were past the point of having to pull each other to the side to compare notes. He looked at Steven still staring at the top of the table. Makani knew that he was now most likely looking at a murderer but would allow Steven to continue playing the role of the grieving newlywed as long as he could.

"We're ready. I'm sorry Steven; it's time," he said standing up and letting Steven walk out the door in front of him leading the way.

Coming up to the overlook Steven began to get nauseous. The two detectives were right behind him and the uniformed officers had begun to use police tape to seal off the area. Steven walked up to the boulders and sat down pointing over to the spot where Gina had fallen.

Both detectives walked towards the edge on opposite sides of the footsteps that were apparently made by Steven and Gina earlier. They have had plenty of experience with accidents, suicides, and people being pushed from the cliffs. It was apparent where she had went over. Each detective knelt down once they reached and edge and looked over then looked at each other.

"I didn't think so. It's been over an hour," said Detective Makani getting up knowing he shouldn't be disappointed that her body wasn't there.

"In today's weather it wouldn't take more than 10 minutes. It's razor sharp down there. With this clearing coming off and that formation at the base it catches hard waves non-stop. It was fast no doubt," said Detective Alamea crossing himself and saying a prayer for Gina.

Instead of standing Alamea turned towards the footprints at the edge and took a small archeologist brush from the inside pocket of his coat. Detective Makani looked around making sure that the area she went over was the only area disturbed.

Detective Alamea began brushing away the loose gravel to reveal the deeper imprints below them. After dusting away the surface he could see where Steven's knees and toes had dug into the ground as he looked over the edge. Just beyond those, was a heal impression that looked like someone that knew they were about to be pushed would be trying to dig in and hang on to solid ground. The way the imprint was facing showed that the cliff and the rocks below had been to this person's back.

"What do you have?" asked Makani bending down.

"Here it looks like the groom got on his knees to look over," said Alamea then changes the focus and points to the heal mark. "And here it looks like someone had their back to the cliff and dug their heal in right before getting knocked off their feet and over the edge."

"And that someone would have been facing someone else standing in that direction," said Makani as he pointed toward Steven and the two looked at each other.

As they both stood up Alamea asks, "What did he say happened this morning?"

"He said it's day one of the honeymoon, he got up and watched the sunrise by himself, made her coffee, says she was up reading or something, he can't remember exactly, then they came hiking and she falls," Makani said raising his eyebrows.

"You're fucking kidding me?" asked Alamea turning his back to Steven so he can't see their expressions.

"That's what he said," replied Makani smiling.

"What a fucking prince. Watches sunrise by himself; hands wife coffee taking no interest in what she's doing; instead of fucking his new bride he wants to go on an 8 miles hike; then new wifey is off the cliff in the first 2 miles. Damn. Sounds like a great fucking honeymoon to me," shaking his head Alamea pulls the journal out of his jacket handing it to Makani.

"What am I looking at?" he asked.

"Last entry. Which is for this morning. If this dumb fuck would have been even half interested in what type of 'reading or something' that she was doing he may have had a chance," Alamea said turning to look at Steven who was pacing back and forth just beyond the boulders.

"Looks like it's time to take a ride," said Makani closing the journal and handing it back to Alamea.

Alamea walked to the scene photographer and pointed to the beginning place he wanted her to start shooting, explaining to follow the prints and do close-ups on the heal imprints in particular.

Makani took point keeping up the façade that she had fallen since they still had 2 miles to get back to their car. He walked up to Steven to get him to think everything was routine.

"Okay Steven. I'm sorry to tell you this but we aren't going to be able to recover Gina's body," said Makani watching his reaction.

Steven looked at him unsure how he was supposed to respond to that. If her body would have been recovered it would have been completely shattered. He was trying to think of how her parents would react. "Ah, okay. I'm sorry I just don't know how I'm going to tell her father."

"We understand Steven, we're going to help you do that. We need you to come with us to the department so that we can start contacting family members and making arrangements," said Makani.

"Sure, okay," said Steven turning to head back down the trail with the detectives behind him.

Detective Makani sat in the interview room with Steven getting him to write down all of Gina's primary family member's contact information. Taking the pad from Steven who has his cell phone in his hand Makani smiles at him.

"Thank you. We'll start with her father first. Can you please show me a picture of Gina?" he asked.

As Steven quickly scrolled through his phone he pulled up a picture of him and Gina a week before the wedding, which was the last time she had been smiling. He turns the phone in his hand and shows it to Makani.

"Steven, I'm sorry but I just need to borrow your phone so that we can make a copy," he said reaching out and taking it from Steven's hand.

"Can't I just e-mail it to you or something?" asked Steven not wanting his phone to leave the room.

"Is there some reason why you don't want me to have your phone?" asked Makani looking directly at Steven questioningly.

Steven picked up quickly that looking like he has something to hide isn't the way to go. "No, sorry, go ahead."

"Excellent. I'll be back shortly. Can I bring you something?" asked Makani.

"A turkey on whole wheat with cucumbers would be great, thank you," said Steven trying to look relaxed.

Trying not to laugh Makani answered, "I'll find a Spam sandwich for you somewhere. Give me a few."

Makani entered the adjacent interview room where they had set up a recorder and a microphone. He walked over and handed Steven's phone to Alamea.

"Did you get the warrant for the phone?" Makani asked him.

"Got it," he replied taking the phone from Makani and handing him pictures of the heal mark in the dirt and copies of the journal entry from that morning. The journal itself was in an evidence bag on the table beside him.

"Nice. Let's see if he was on the phone like Gina wrote," said Makani watching Alamea pull up the call log.

At 7:37am there was an outgoing call to a contact named Hanie Industries. Makani smiled at Alamea and said, "Would you like to do the honors?"

"Why yes I would," replied Alamea smiling at him.

Makani wrote down Hanie Industries on the legal pad then started the recording device. Alamea pressed the number to call it then placed it on speaker. It only took one ring for Stephanie to answer.

"Baby!!! Tell me how much you love and miss this pussy!" she cooed on the other end.

Both men were quiet waiting to see how much she would say before they interrupted. They were hoping for an "is she dead" question to implicate her. Makani tapped the pad and showed Alamea he had written 'Step' to the left of Hanie which spelled Stephanie.

"Babe are you there? What's wrong did she walk in the room?" she asked talking quieter than before.

"Actually Stephanie this is Detective Alamea and with me is Detective Makani. We need to ask you a few questions," he said as they looked at each other expecting her to hang up the phone.

There was a heavy silence on the other end. Stephanie took several moments before answering, "I'm sorry, where is Steven?" she asked with her voice quivering.

"He's unavailable at the moment, sorry Stephanie. I need you to verify the nature of the conversation you had with him this morning at 7:37am," said Alameda.

After another moment of silence she answered, "I can't remember exactly."

"Can you tell me what your relationship is to Steven?" asked Alamea.

"He just married my best friend Gina," she answered slowly.

"So why was he calling you at 7:37 in the morning instead of Gina?" he asked.

"You know what, I remember now, he called to ask me where he should take Gina for lunch," she said hurriedly.

"Why would he need your help with that? Especially when you're four time zones away," asked Alamea.

"Well, that's kind of my thing. I helped them book that honeymoon. Found that condo for them and everything. I know what restaurants and sites are within 25 miles of that location," she said gaining momentum as bits of the truth were giving her something to grab onto.

"Any particular reason why you chose a honeymoon location with a cliff instead of a beach Stephanie?" Alamea asked with a sharper tone.

The two detectives looked at each other as Stephanie's silence said volumes to them.

"What's going on? When can I talk to Steven?" she asked nervously.

"Why is it that you're only asking to speak to Steven? Where is it that you think Gina is if not here with us?" asked Alamea.

"Okay fine, Gina. You're calling me from his phone that's all," she replied flustered.

"So here's the thing Stephanie; Steven won't be coming to the phone for a while. Who will be calling however, is someone from your local law enforcement agency. My suggestion to you is to cooperate with them fully or call an attorney. Be sure to stay close to your phone. We'll be in touch," said Alamea as he hung up the phone.

Makani stopped the recording, looked at Alamea and smiled. "She found the condo for them and everything," he said mocking her.

"Fucking priceless," said Makani. He let out a sigh then stood up flipping through the pictures of the crime scene and of Gina's journal. "You wouldn't happen to have a turkey on wheat with cucumber would you?"

The two detectives laughed as they left the room.

Makani and Alamea walked into the interview room ready to let Steven know it was time to drop the act. Steven was sitting at the table and looked nervous as they walked in together.

"Sorry Steven I couldn't find a sandwich," said Makani sitting down in the chair across from him. "What I do have for you, is some pictures and questions."

Alamea stood in the corner watching and holding the pictures of the journal entry from the morning. He wanted to be the one sitting in front of Steven when he read it.

Makani put three pictures of the ground at the edge of the cliff on the table. He watched Steven study the pictures longer than someone whose wife had simply fallen off a cliff. Makani touched the middle one that had the close up of the heal print and slid it towards him.

"What do you think made that mark right there?" asked Makani pointing at the heal print.

"I assume a foot," said Steven looking at Makani and then at Alamea trying to get a feel for them.

"A foot would be correct," he said firmly at Steven. "More specifically, it's a heal print."

Steven looked at Makani confused and said, "Okay?"

"Tell me one more time how she fell off the cliff," Makani asked sitting back in his chair and crossing his arms.

"We had stopped to drink some water. She walked over to look at the rocks at the bottom of the cliff and she fell over," Steven said becoming more emotional and nervous.

Makani leaned forward looking at him. "I thought that's what you had said. The problem with that version of your story though Steven, is that if she would've been looking over the cliff and had fallen face first, then there would be toe impressions or tracks where her toes or balls of her feet slipped. The back of her feet, meaning her heals, wouldn't even be on the ground most likely."

Makani paused and looked at Steven shift in his chair before continuing, "See these beautiful cliffs attract people from all over the world. I'd rather not put a number on the amount of deaths associated with them, but let's just say that I've seen enough to know that when someone accidentally falls off the cliff they either go face first, or perhaps they slip and slide off sideways, something of that nature." He stopped long enough to tap the picture again and kept focusing on Steven as he watched him begin to lose the grip on his bullshit story.

"See this heal mark here? This tells me that Gina's back was to the cliffs when she lost her balance and went over. The only thing she would have been facing, would be you," Makani stated firmly.

Steven's mind began spinning. He was trying to decide if he should tell them what really happened. He could feel small beads of sweet on his upper lip as he remembered Gina's face before she let herself fall backwards off the cliff.

"I don't know what you expect me to say. I told you what happened," Steven said pushing the picture back towards Makani trying to get the image of Gina to leave his mind.

Makani looked over his shoulder at Alamea standing in the corner. Knowing that he was ready to take over Makani got out of the chair and they switched places. Alamea stacked the three pictures of the edge on top of each other with the close-up of the heal print on top. He pushed them to the side but kept his pictures to himself for a moment.

"Remind us what you told my partner that your wife was doing when you brought her coffee this morning," said Alamea looking intently at Steven.

"She was reading," he said looking back and forth between the two detectives.

"Are you sure she was reading Steven?" asked Alamea knowing that he was going to enjoy watching Steven ride the roller coaster he was about to put him on.

"I think so. I don't remember exactly. What difference does it make?" he asked getting agitated.

"It makes a big difference Steven," said Alamea wondering if Steven was really that shallow to not know that Gina had written about the entire affair from the day she had seen them in Stephanie's back yard in her journal. She had left nothing out.

"Did Gina keep a journal?" Alamea asked Steven.

"If you mean one specific journal I couldn't tell you. She has spirals, books, journals, everywhere, all over the place. She's never without one. She makes lists about how to breathe in the morning, it's non-stop with her. So, when I gave her the coffee she had some type of book or journal or whatever but I didn't pay attention to what it was," Steven said frustrated.

"You know for a man on the first day of his honeymoon I'm not hearing the love Steven. My partner showed me Gina's picture and she's stunning. First of all, I would have taken my beautiful bride out of bed to look at the sunrise with me, not left her alone. Secondly, I would've brought her coffee, taken whatever she was holding out of her hands and laid her on the bed to enjoy the first day as my wife. But that's just me," said Alamea watching Steven's reaction.

Steven was trying to control his anger. He was still clinging to the hope that they weren't going to turn this into a suicide and expose his affair. He knew he didn't push Gina off the cliff so he was trying to push the fear that they were accusing him of it out of his mind. He didn't want to look guilty but the guilt of the affair and what it had done to Gina was beginning to set in as he again looked back and forth between the two detectives becoming increasingly nervous.

"Did you make any calls this morning?" asked Alamea.

Steven stirred in his seat and looked at Makani. He didn't know what to say. He had to assume that they had looked at his phone since Makani had taken it.

"Yes, I had to make a business call," said Steven clearing his voice.

"And what was the nature of that business call?" he asked.

"It had to do with stocks and market shares. I don't expect you to understand why I would make a call like that on such an important day, but it was necessary," said Steven on the offensive.

Alamea smiled and paused taking in Steven's arrogance knowing that Steven was riding up the first hill of the roller coaster. He thinks he has a great view and knows what to expect when they go racing down the track. As with most riders, he had no idea.

"And the name of that company is?" asked Alamea raising his eyebrows.

"Hanie Industries," said Steven knowing that if they checked his call log that would be the honest answer.

"Detective Makani would you mind getting the recording from next door?" asked Alamea turning to him in the corner.

As Makani leaves the room Alamea leans forward and asks Steven, "Tell me about Stephanie."

Steven froze as her name hit his ears. This was exactly what he didn't want to happen.

"She's my wife's best friend. She's like her sister," he said avoiding asking why.

"What I would like to know, is who is Stephanie to you?" asked Alamea as Makani walked back in the room and put the recorder on the table in between them.

"She's nobody to me. She's always around and is practically Gina's shadow. She's like family," he said extremely nervous about what was just placed on the table.

Makani stood at the table and looked at Steven's chest and neck turn red. He looked like he was ready to break out in hives.

"So after we took care of Gina's picture we were required to check your call log. We did see that you made a call to Hanie Industries at 7:37am. Until Gina's death is classified we follow all leads so we were also required to make a call to Hanie Industries to determine the nature of your call this morning. This is the recording of that call," said Makani pressing play.

The sound of Stephanie's voice instantly echoed off the walls, *"Baby!!! Tell me how much you love and miss this pussy!"* Makani reached down and stopped the recording and stared at Steven with a 'time to cut the shit' look.

"To repeat my last question; who is Stephanie to you?" Alamea asked Steven who went from being red to turning pale.

Steven began to realize that this was turning into hostile questioning. He didn't even want to know what else Stephanie had said. He had no idea what to say or how to continue.

"Is she your tour guide? She did mention that she's the one that found the condo for you and Gina. Curious that your mistress would place your new bride above a cliff instead of on a cozy beach," said Alamea watching Steven begin to shut down. He knew he didn't have much longer before he asked for an attorney.

"I find it curious," said Makani staring down at Steven. He began walking around the table keeping his eyes on Steven. "Even more curious that instead of turning to your new bride and making love to her you got out of bed and made a call to Stephanie. The person that, according to her, knows everything about this area for 25 miles. Curious that instead of making love to your wife you're on the phone comparing notes with your lover before you head off on the 8 mile trail. You were very specific about knowing that the overlook was exactly 2 miles in. Extremely curious that your wife happens to 'fall' at the very first place you stop don't you think?" he asked stopping back in front of the table.

"What I find curious, is that your wife has told us more about you and Stephanie after her death than you probably ever will," said Alamea handing Steven the copy of the morning's journal entry from Gina.

"What's this?" asked Steven.

"We'd like for you to read it out loud," said Alamea.

Steven began reading it slowly, "*This morning I awoke to find Steven's side of the bed empty. Knowing it was our first day as husband and wife I wanted to find him and see if I could put the affair out of my mind, at least for the day. I walked through the condo looking for him and heard his voice coming from the bathroom off the main living space. I listened at the door and now I'm terrified and devastated. Yes I know of their affair but I never thought that two people I loved so much would conspire to kill me,*" Steven paused as the last words take him aback. He blinked and continued to read simply out of sheer curiosity and knowing that he didn't conspire to kill her.

"*I heard Steven tell Stephanie that he would push me off the cliff at the first place we rest. That alone shattered me, but then I could tell that Stephanie was coaching him on when to do it and how to do it. I heard him saying that he would make sure that rocks below would be jagged enough to break my body apart and make it part of the ocean. I can't believe I didn't think of this sooner,*" Steven threw the paper on the table and began yelling, "That's complete bullshit!"

"Bullshit? Which part exactly? The part about her going off of the cliff the first time you stop to rest?" asked Alamea picking up the paper to continue.

"You didn't finish Steven. Let me help: *Stephanie had everything to do with picking this location for our honeymoon. I repeatedly told both her and Steven that I wanted a sweet little hut on the beach and instead we end up at the top of a cliff in 2,000 square feet that's anything but romantic. Why didn't I see this sooner? Now unless I can over-power Steven, today will be my last day. My hands are shaking, I'm not ready to die. I'm not ready.*"

Steven slammed his hand on the top of the table enraged! He remembered Gina's face as she looked at him and told him she was twice as smart as he was. She had everything planned before they even started for that hike.

"She's a fucking liar!" he yelled no longer able to control himself.

"Why don't you just tell us how you pushed her off the cliff Steven," said Makani.

"I didn't fucking push her she jumped!" he screamed at them.

Makani and Alamea look at each amused.

"She jumped? Wow really? The same Gina that had just written that she wasn't ready to die?" asked Alamea.

"The same Gina that you said slipped and fell while looking over the edge?" asked Makani.

"Yes the same fucking Gina! She's wicked fucking smart okay. She must have heard me on the phone with Stephanie and plotted this shit out," Steven said so pissed off he couldn't control his emotions.

"I think it's pretty obvious that she heard you on the phone with Stephanie," said Makani watching Steven become infuriated.

"You know what I mean! I wasn't saying anything about Gina on the phone. I was just talking to Stephanie about sex, that's it. So, fine, I'm a piece of shit, but I didn't bring Gina here to throw her off a cliff! I came here to start my life with her," he said.

"You know that would be a hell of a lot more convincing if you had actually acted like a husband this morning. I mean we don't have her body. You could have easily said that you made mad passionate love to her before you went on the hike. But, you didn't. You admitted that your goal this morning was to get her on that trail as soon as possible," said Alamea.

"Here's the thing Steven," said Makani pushing the picture of the heal print back in front of him. "People that jump off a cliff to kill themselves always go face first."

"I have to second that," said Alamea. "Suicide is very personal. People committing suicide usually stare at the place their body will be laying for hours sometimes before finally jumping."

"Gina went over that cliff backwards," said Makani pointing to the heal print.

"Yeah she did! She fucking put her arms out and just let herself fall backwards. I tried to stop her. I tried, I did, but she was so pissed about Stephanie that she wouldn't listen to me. She just fucking fell backwards," Steven said looking at them and expecting them to believe him since he was telling the truth.

"This right here, shows that she was knocked off balance backwards. Aside from that, you've been bullshitting us all day long until we hand you Gina's own handwriting saying she would be dead from falling from a cliff by the end of the day. If she truly killed herself you should have told us from the jump," said Makani.

"This will go much easier on you with a full confession. Stephanie is going to be answering these same questions so keep that in mind before you let another lie come out of your mouth," said Alamea.

"I need to call my attorney," said Steven staring at them coldly as he crossed his arms and refused to say another word.

Steven sat at the defense table on trial for First Degree Murder. Detective Alamea took the stand and looked over at him hoping that he would get the maximum sentence allowed. He was sworn in then the Prosecutor handed him the copy of the journal entry and asked him to read it. When he was finished he looked at the jury and was satisfied that they felt the same way he had the first time he had read it.

Stephanie sat at the defense table on trial for Conspiracy to Commit Murder. Detective Alamea took the stand once again and read Gina's journal entry. This time to implicate Stephanie in Gina's murder. When he finished reading the entry he was then asked to verify that he was present for the recording of Stephanie answering the call he had made to Hanie Industries. As they played the recording Stephanie put her face in her hands and cried.

With a full courtroom it was time to hear the verdict. Steven looked at the jury hoping that they somehow saw the truth in the lies that Gina had woven before she killed herself. He recalled how smug he had felt as he tore her to shreds with his words after she had said she was smarter than him. Although he knew he was innocent of pushing her off of the cliff, he also knew that it was ultimately because of him that she went over it. He had the past year to replay it over and over again in his mind. All he had to do was try harder to get her to enjoy the honeymoon and instead she had played to his weakness, his ego, and she had won.

"Will the defendant please rise," stated the Judge. As Steven rose to his feet he continued, "Has the jury reached a verdict?"

"Yes your honor," stated the foreman.

"What say you?" asked the Judge.

"In the charge of Murder in the First Degree, we the jury find the defendant, Guilty."

Stephanie stood up and tried to steady herself against the table. Knowing that she may be about to go to prison for something she didn't do, all while losing everyone that was ever close to her, was more than she felt she could bear.

"Has the jury reached a verdict?" asked the Judge.

"Yes your honor," stated the foreman.

"What say you one and all?" asked the Judge.

"In the charge of Conspiracy to Commit Murder, we find the defendant, Guilty."

Mary

Marshall Simmons watched Mary's trailer come into view as they wound around the dirt road that had taken them over five miles into the woods from the main road. Sheriff Becker was driving and had been describing what little he knew about George to the Marshall.

"Like I said I've only had a few run-ins with George over the years. His kin has owned this land since before I was around. He works in the mines and comes home and keeps to himself. Just a couple times he's been at a bar and I've been called on those occasions. George isn't the type of man to stay calm in an intense situation. I wish my deputy wasn't off fishing or you would have brought someone else. I did put my vest on for this, just so you know. Once he realizes that we mean to put him in handcuffs he's going to go ape shit," the Sheriff shook his head back and forth anticipating what was to come.

"My only response to that is this; he leaves here alive. I'll take point when he gets here. You fall back and follow up if needed, but I'm ready for old George and his tantrums," said the Marshall as they pulled up to the trailer.

The two men exit the car and look around the property before deciding where to start. George was still at work, which was what they wanted. They needed to search the property without him seeing them pull up or expecting them to be there. They had waited until they had the search warrant in hand and it had been verified that he was at work.

Marshall Simmons looked closely at the shed knowing that the anti-freeze was most likely in it, but his first priority was to find Mary's glass. He pointed to the trailer and motioned for the Sheriff to follow him.

He pulled two pair of latex gloves from a pouch on his belt then handed one pair to the Sheriff and began putting his on before he reached for the door handle.

Simmons pulled open the screen door and tried the handle on the heavy door which swung open immediately. As soon as the door opened the sound of flies and the smell of rotten food hit them both hard.

Walking through the small living area they had to step over beer bottles that were all over the place. The kitchen was just to the left and there were trash and dishes piled all over the counter and in the sink. The table was littered with beer bottles and trash thrown on top of it.

"We're looking for a clear glass that has yellow flowers on it," said Simmons as he went to the table and began peeling back the layers of junk food trash that were on it.

"You got it," said the Sheriff walking over to the sink and beginning to sift through the dishes and trash there.

Simmons threw a pizza box to the floor revealing a plate full of food that was now covered in flies. It also looked to be splattered with blood and vomit. He knew that Mary must have gotten dinner on the table before finally collapsing which didn't surprise him. As he moved the carton to a 12 pack out of the way he sees Mary's glass laid over on its side with what looks like tobacco spit across the side of it.

"Here we go," Simmons said lifting it up with one hand and pulling an evidence bag out of his inner jacket pocket. He was careful to keep the little bit of liquid that was resting on the side of the glass from spilling out.

"I got the bag," said Becker taking the bag from him and helping him get the glass and the liquid in the bag and sealed.

"Thank you George for being such an arrogant bastard that you didn't even bother to try and wash away the evidence," said Simmons with a smile on his face.

As Becker logs the time they collected the evidence Simmons walks to the back of the trailer. There is a small bathroom that holds only male brand toiletries. He does find some feminine pads in the cabinet below the sink with a toothbrush shoved into the box.

In the bedroom the bed and dresser take up almost the whole space. The only closet they have has George's clothes in it and his shoes in the bottom. Simmons looked around looking for any sign of Mary's things and can visually see nothing. He wondered if George got rid of her things in anger but dismissed that because there are no empty spaces that look to be where Mary's things would've been kept. Everything looked to be where it had been for years.

Simmons walks over to the dresser and begins opening the drawers. In the bottom drawer were women's clothing that appeared to be old and worn out. There were enough garments for only three days of clothing. Slowly shutting the drawer Simmons rose to his feet and fought back tears for Mary. It was apparent that she had been treated no better than a dog that gets kicked and beat by its owner. Just by looking through the trailer there was no trace of Mary and who she was.

Walking back into the kitchen area Becker was finished sealing and logging the glass in the evidence bag. Simmons walks past him for the front door ready to look in the shed.

Entering the shed and looking around the two men look at each other frowning. On the ground alone were around 10 bottles of anti-freeze and there were two bottles on the bench.

"Damn Marshall, I don't think we brought enough evidence bags," said the Sheriff pushing his hat to the top of his head.

"We're going to start with the two that are on the bench," said Simmons walking towards it. He looked at the bottle that is clearly covered in large, smudged oily fingerprints and dirt. He knew they would have no problem pulling prints from anything in the shed because George obviously never had clean hands. He also knew all he needed was this bottle in front of him. He didn't plan on bothering with anything else.

As the Sheriff helps Simmons place the anti-freeze container in an evidence bag they can hear a truck roaring up the main road towards them. The Sheriff is immediately alarmed.

"Marshall I can guarantee you he has a shotgun and a rifle in his truck. We don't want him getting the jump on us," said the Sheriff as the two men draw their weapons and walk out of the shed ready for him to come up the drive.

As George spotted them he sped up his truck as if threatening to run them over. They saw him reach back with his right hand and grab his shotgun off the rack behind his head. He clearly put the butt toward the floorboard and cocked it.

"Hold up the warrant and stay out of range," said Simmons as he walked in front of the Sheriff, raised his weapon and shot out George's tire making the truck start to spin.

George threw down the shotgun and grabbed the steering wheel trying to control the truck. He kept it from rolling then hopped out and pulled the shotgun from the seat pointing it at Simmons.

"What the fuck is this? You're on private property you need to get the fuck out of here," yelled George.

Simmons took a stance behind their car. He knew that it wasn't a question of "if" George would pull on him, he knew it was "when". And the fact that George was holding a shotgun didn't put a smile on his face.

"We have a warrant to search your property and your vehicle George. We're just here to do our civic duty," said Simmons with his weapon still pointed at George.

George spit and sneered at him, "Civic duty my ass. I pay taxes. Get the fuck off my property. I know my rights."

"You do? Excellent. Let's talk some more about your rights. We're here to arrest you for Attempted Murder George. So, basically you have the right to remain silent, the right to.."

"Fuck you! Attempted murder my ass! That stupid bitch was passed out on the floor when I got home from work. I didn't do shit!" he screamed becoming more confident in the thought that he hadn't tried to kill her.

"You mean to say you haven't been slipping Mary a little anti-freeze to top off her lemonade?" asked Simmons.

"What the fuck is this? What kind of mess are you talkin?" asked George confused.

"I'm talking about the fact that you have Mary knocking on heaven's door from drinking your poison lemonade. That's what the fuck I'm talking about. Ring a bell George?" asked Simmons taking small steps sideways keeping their car between him and George's shotgun pellets that could come any second.

"You're a fucking idiot. I don't know what you're trying to pull but it don't matter no way. Mary is my wife. I can do with her what I want," spat George becoming more irritated that he still didn't understand what was happening.

Images of the pictures of Mary's wounds flashed into Simmons mind and he wanted to shoot George in the face. He knew that George truly believed that Mary was nothing more than an object that he owned and could do with as he wished.

"Yeah here's the thing with that George; no you can't. Aside from the fact that it's morally and ethically wrong to treat your wife like an object that you can abuse at will, there are laws in place that make it illegal for you to 'do with her what you want'. Mary has been severely beaten and poisoned over the last month and you're the only person she's been in contact with during that time. For that reason you are being charged with Attempted Murder," said Simmons knowing that George was not about to go with them quietly.

George licked his lips and looked over at the sheriff. "Becker you gonna let this dumb fucker die today for not knowin whose property he's on?"

"You need to come with us George. Put the gun down," said the Sheriff also pointing his weapon at George.

"Well ain't this some serious bullshit! I don't do nothin but work my fuckin ass off for that bitch and this is what I get in return? What the fuck! I didn't do shit to her," George screamed testing the water one last time to see if he could talk his way out of it.

"George, you can cut the shit. You're going down today. Mary is about to get her retribution for putting up with your sadistic country ass. Your only option is to put down your weapon, allow us to handcuff you, and enjoy the ride to the station," said Simmons calmly.

"Or I could just shoot you two muther fuckers then set you on fire while I go inside and enjoy my beer," said George.

"Okay then, second option would be to get a ride to the hospital first, get treated for gunshot wounds, then go to the station. Your choice," said Simmons ready to fire.

George looked back and forth between the two men pointing their weapons at him. He didn't understand exactly what was going on with Mary but he did understand that he was going to jail for a very long time if he went down for what they were saying and he wasn't about to let that happen.

As George's face twisted he narrowed his eyes and kept his weapon pointed at Simmons, gripped his shotgun a little tighter and started to pull the trigger. Before George can get off a round Simmons puts a bullet in his left shoulder then right knee. George dropped the shotgun and fell to the ground screaming and cursing.

"I see you chose option 2," said Simmons.

He walked up to George and grabbed the shotgun unloading it while George writhes in pain in front of him. When he's finished he bends down to talk loud enough that only George can hear him.

"I just want you to know that I have people inside the prison. I'm going to have them give you a scar for every scar of Mary's before they start giving you points for your own. Do you know how many scars she has? From the tip of her toes to the top of her head she has 258 scars from your sorry ass. I'm going to be sure that you feel every one of them," winked Simmons as he stood up and waited for Becker to help him get George in the car.

Mary stood outside the courtroom shaking. She was to testify against George and was waiting to be called in. She hadn't laid eyes on him since the day she was taken from the trailer. Marshall Simmons stood with her outside the doors to escort her in when they were ready.

"Okay Mary. Now you know that we have plenty of evidence that George did this but you need to expect for his attorney to try and spin this in their favor. He's still sticking to the story that you poisoned yourself. We know you didn't so just hold tight to the facts and you'll be fine," he said smiling and trying to give her confidence.

The Mary that was standing outside the courtroom was not the same Mary of six months earlier. She had color and looked healthy. She smiled back at him then reached down and squeezed her purse feeling herself fill with confidence.

As Simmons opened the doors for her, Mary had to take a deep breath then exhale before being able to walk forward through the doors. As she walked down the courtroom towards the stand she tried to keep from trembling. She was in a daze as she was sworn in. She kept her back to George and didn't look at him.

On the stand as Mary answered the Prosecutors questions she was emotional and embarrassed having to recount years of abuse that had her blanketed in shame for years. Members of the jury had even begun to cry.

Mary was then asked to recount the evening with the life insurance policy increase. She then stated that approximately a month later was when she noticed her lemonade had become increasingly sweet.

"So Mary is it correct in saying that it was only after George had increased the life insurance policy on you that you began to notice your lemonade being sweeter than it had ever been before?" he asked.

"That's correct," stated Mary. For an instant she looked over at George to see his reaction to what he had to now know was her finally beating him.

George slams his fist on the table and screams as loud as he can, "She did it herself! She did all this!"

The Judge slams the gavel down trying to get control of the courtroom as everyone has started buzzing at George's outburst.

"Order in the court!" he yelled until he had control again. "Mr. Davis if your client has another outburst he will be held in contempt and removed from the courtroom."

"Yes your honor," stated Defense Attorney Davis.

As everyone calmed down Mary began to get the courage to not only look at George again, but to stare him down. She couldn't remember the last time she had looked him in the eyes because it infuriated him, but now was her time.

As Mary looked at George and began to raise her head up and wipe her tears he lost control of his emotions. George refused to be disrespected by Mary regardless of who was watching and although he hadn't tried to kill her, he wanted to kill her at that moment.

"You stupid fucking bitch!" screamed George as he stood up and grabbed the glass from the table in front of him and threw it at her. Glass and water shattered all over Mary and the Judge as George jumped the table headed for Mary. Bailiffs tackle George as he's screaming and fighting and the Judge pulls Mary from the stand and puts her behind him as George is removed from the courtroom.

The day of sentencing George is walked into the courtroom by two bailiffs with both his arms and legs shackled. Mary sits in the back of the courtroom watching him enter. She had so many mixed emotions. In a strange way she felt sorry for him. She had struggled with tinges of guilt over the past few months. Yet as she attended more therapy sessions, had more meetings, and met more people, she had begun to realize that no part of her life had been normal. Not knowing what normal was had distorted her perception of right and wrong. Anytime she felt sorry for him she would look in the mirror. Something she could never do when she had been with him. At that point she would remember that he had put her through pure hell for three decades and he had everything coming to him that he was going to get.

"Jury have you reached a verdict," asked the Judge looking down his nose at George.

"We have your honor," stated the jury Foreman.

"How do you find?" asked the Judge.

Before they announce the verdict George turns and looks for Mary in the courtroom. As he spots her his eyes project so much hate that

Mary's breath catches and she can feel it from where she stands. Instead of looking away, she says a prayer under her breath thankful that she would get to see his face as the verdict was read. Then she smiled at him.

"For the charge of Attempted Murder, we the jury find the Defendant, Guilty."

Calvin

Detective Andrews and Detective Marlo are pulling down the street to what is already a chaotic mess. The house had been taped off and officers were now in the street barricading it to keep neighbors and the onset of media arriving back away from the open window and what was lying inside.

"And so it begins," said Marlo slowing and trying to decide where to park.

"Since we're dealing with the husband I'm assuming you want me to take point with him," she said. They decided that in situations like this the subject does better with the opposite sex. She would sit with the husband while her partner walked the scene.

"Yes ma'am. Do your thing," he said pulling over and parking.

After getting out the two detectives walked up to the Sergeant on the scene to get a briefing.

"Detectives," he said nodding and shaking their hands. "The husband Jason is in the bedroom. We haven't been able to get him to come out. Apparently he found her after he came home from a racquetball game. Says he walked over to the area the body was laying but didn't go near her because he could tell she was already dead. He then proceeded to the bedroom to lock himself in the room and call 911. He has blood on the bottom of his shoes but not a lot of it. Apparently he stepped in spatter before getting close enough to her to see the body. Neighbors are saying that they didn't hear anything until he started screaming her name a little after 9pm."

"So no sounds of a struggle or altercation of any kind?" asked Andrews.

"No ma'am not at this time. We've talked to the immediate neighbors but we're still canvasing the block. I have officers going through the alley so we'll have an update to you on that here shortly," said the Sergeant.

"Excellent thank you Sergeant," said Marlo motioning for Andrews to enter the house in front of him. Before they walked inside they stopped and put booties on their feet. The blood spatter from the body was all the way to within five feet of the front door.

Walking over to the body Andrews squats down to get a closer look. She had to stop counting at 15 stab wounds. There was too much blood and exposed skin to be able to tell exactly how many wounds the victim had until she was cleaned and examined.

"I'm guessing she was sitting down when she was attacked. It looks like she just slumped over and fell out of the chair," said Marlo standing behind the chair to get a better view.

"Well she may have been sitting down calmly but whoever did this was pissed off. It's been a long time since we've seen something this angry," said Andrews nodding her head in agreement and looking around the room to the walls and then ceiling.

"You go find Jason and I'll take a stroll through and see what I see," said Marlo standing still but turning around to see what is directly behind him to determine which way the killer would have walked.

It looked as though the bloody footprints from the body lead over to the rug the dining room table sits on where the killer apparently wiped their feet. There were a few faint footprints leading from the rug to the kitchen but only a few. The prints appeared to be men's athletic shoes somewhere between a 10 and a 12. They would have to measure to be certain.

Andrews goes through the hallway and nods to the uniform officer standing outside the door. She knocks and enters when Jason answers. He's sitting on the bed with his phone beside him looking distraught.

"Hello Jason, I'm Detective Andrews. I'm sorry for your loss," she said walking closer to him so that she could try to get a good read on his face when she began questioning him.

"Thank you," said Jason clearly shaken. He did not have any blood on his skin or clothing. Simply on the bottom of his shoes. He is wearing a suit but she remembered the Sergeant saying that he said he had come from a racquetball game.

"I need you to tell me what happened this evening," she said leaving it open for Jason to start where he felt appropriate. Not giving a specific timeline question to answer usually throws off guilty parties because they're expecting to account for their time minute by minute from the time questioning starts. Andrews knows it's much smarter to let them jump around. Jumping back to a lie that is thin usually results in falling through the ice.

"I don't know what happened. I came home and walked in from the garage and there she was. That's it," he said looking dazed and confused.

"So walk me through coming home Jason. You just said 'there she was'. You told the operator that your wife was dead when you placed the call to us. How did you determine that she was dead?" she asked looking him over.

"Are you fucking kidding me? Unless something has changed from the last time I was in there her fucking blood is covering the place and I don't even know what the fuck happened to her body, it's just…….fucked up," he said not having any words he needed to help the situation. He hadn't gotten close enough to her to know exactly what her wounds were.

Andrews imagined the man in front of her looking at his wife and deciding that she was too "fucked up" to get dirty to try and figure out if she had any kind of a chance left so he ran his punk ass back to the bedroom to call for help without getting his clothes dirty. To her that meant he either truly was a huge vagina or he wanted his wife dead and knew she was dead so no need to confirm, get dirty, or double check.

"Okay then. To make sure I'm getting your statement down correctly; you came home, walked in from the garage, saw your wife on the floor with her blood everywhere, determined that she was too 'fucked up' to check her for a pulse or any sign of life, then you ran back here to lock yourself in the room and call 911. Did I miss anything?" she asked wanting to knock the hell out of him.

Detective Marlo had been examining the back door in the kitchen for signs of forced entry. The door was unlocked but he knew that there had been officers already searching the back yard and alley so they could have left it open. Either way the lock wasn't broken and the door frame looked perfect.

He walked out onto the back porch and around the perimeter of the house. He noted that all of the windows were intact. No sign of forced entry via window. There were also no signs of footprints or anything out of the ordinary. The night had been dry and he knew the chances of prints being left behind were slim unless they had landscaping that would have captured it. There were a pile of broken leaves under the windows on the side of the house which unfortunately, don't hold the shape of prints.

Walking back in the kitchen from the backdoor a trail of water on the floor was capturing the light and caught his eye. It was from the sink to the back door. He slowly stepped to the side of the trail and followed it over to the sink. He looked in the sink and noticed a few spatters of blood on the side of it. His eyes then followed the water from the sink, to the countertop, and up and onto the knife set sitting so boldly on the counter.

"You've got to be fucking kidding me," said Marlo using his gloved hand to pull the wet knife from its place in the set. Although the knife had been recently cleaned there was still traces of blood where the blade met the handle. The cleaning job had been very sloppy and very fast.

Smiling Marlo looks from the knife set and the water does go from it, back to the counter then down to the floor and out the back door. Not seconds later a uniformed officer walks through the back door with a duffle bag in his gloved hands.

"Detective," he said nodding to Marlo. "I assume you're who I need to give this to?"

"It's Christmas in October, this is awesome," he said placing the knife gently on the counter then reaching out for the bag. "Please get me an evidence bag for this knife and I need this whole set and holder bagged up. Can you also send in the photographer so we can get shots before we get it sealed up?"

"Yes sir," stated the officer as he went towards the front of the house.

Marlo opened the bag to reveal bloody clothing and a pair of bloody workout shoes. Men's size 11.5.

Jason had begun to get an attitude with Andrews once he realized that her questioning towards him was anything but what it should have been to a grieving husband.

"Look you don't have to be a bitch to me okay. That's my fucking wife laying in there dead so cut the attitude," he snapped at her.

Andrews smiled at him. She loved nothing more than getting under the skin of anyone she was questioning. She was becoming convinced that Jason was anything but grieving.

"Yes I saw her. I couldn't tell you exactly how many wounds she has but I can tell you that in my experience she was killed by someone that knew her personally. Crimes of passion are always more violent and full of rage," she said studying his reaction.

"What's that supposed to mean?" he snapped at her defensively.

"Who do you know that hates your wife on that level?" she asked plainly.

"No one. I don't know. She doesn't know anyone or go anywhere I don't think," he said with his mind racing trying to truly figure out who could have done this to her. He had been thinking that it had to be one of his mistresses but he wasn't ready to share that.

"Where were you playing racquetball and who were you playing with?" she asked taking him from an emotional question to a factual question and ready to stir him up.

"What do you mean?" he asked getting flustered. He hadn't told her that he had been playing racquetball and he was beginning to think that he shouldn't use that story because it was obviously bullshit.

"I mean that when we got here the Sergeant on scene told us that you told him that you had just come home from playing racquetball," she said looking over his clothing again.

"Right. Right," he said putting his head in his hands and leaning over the bed as he began to feel ill.

"So where was this game?" she asked again.

"All right. All right. I know this doesn't look good but I wasn't playing racquetball," he said running his hands through his hair as he sat up trying to get a handle on the situation.

"Why did you tell the Sergeant that you were?" she asked beginning to document his statements and the exact times he stated them in her notepad.

"Because I was going to. But my bag was stolen from my car so I didn't go. I was just thinking that it's Wednesday and that's what I do on Wednesday so that was my auto response," he said flustered.

"Your auto-response?" she asked confused.

"Yes," he nodded.

"How did they break into your car and when did you report it?" she asked looking at him questioningly.

Jason looked at her nervously not wanting to answer. "I didn't have time to report it."

"You didn't have time? Well, I'm here now, how'd they break into your car?" she asked.

"I don't know my bag was just missing," he said getting frustrated.

"Uh huh. So your car was broken into, your bag was stolen, but you don't know how?" she said taking notes making him more upset.

"The bag was in my back seat when I went into work this morning and it was gone when I came out," he said.

"No broken windows, locks, nothing?" she asked.

"No," he said looking at her like he wanted to slap her.

"So where were you this evening? Where did you go that kept you too busy to report the theft of your belongings?" she asked.

"I was with a colleague having drinks," he said.

Just as Andrews is about to start digging in with more questions she hears Marlo clear his throat in the hallway and he motions for her to come out of the room.

"Hold that thought," she said as she walked away from Jason and into the hallway.

Walking down the hall the two detectives go further towards the living room so that they can talk without being heard.

"What's your feeling?" asked Marlo.

"I feel like he's a piece of shit that would rather his wife die than give her CPR and get his clothes dirty," said Andrews.

"What would you say if I told you we have a bloody knife in the kitchen and a bag full of bloody clothes that was dumped in the alley; men's athletic clothes to be specific."

"I'd say it's Christmas in October," she said.

"That's what I fucking said!" he said laughing. She smiled and shook her head looking back towards the bedroom.

"Okay then. I take it we can continue our conversation at the precinct. I knew he was a dumbass but damn," she said heading back in the room to arrest Jason with Marlo following her.

On the stand in the courtroom was LeAnn's sister, Rebecca. She was crying and testifying about the phone conversation she was having with LeAnn the night of her murder.

"Would you please recount the conversation you had with your sister the evening she was killed?" asked the Prosecutor.

"It was around 6:30 in the evening. I know we talked for at least an hour," she said wiping her tears.

"And please tell the court what you and LeAnn were discussing," he asked.

"She told me that she had started to think that Jason had been having an affair on Wednesdays. There had been several things over the past few months that had happened to make her suspicious," said Rebecca.

"Was that the first time that LeAnn had told you that she felt Jason was cheating on her?" he asked.

"No sir it wasn't," she said shaking her head no.

"What was different about this time Rebecca?" he asked calmly knowing that the answer would upset her.

"She said that when he got home she was going to confront him about it," said Rebecca beginning to cry so hard that she couldn't continue.

Although Jason had been advised by counsel not to take the stand, his arrogance wasn't going to let him go through an entire trial without having his say. The Prosecutor had already been making a meal out of Jason and was smiling as he continued to do so.

"We'd like you to name for the court all of the people that hated your wife LeAnn to the point that they would be compelled to stab her 27 times," he said looking at Jason.

"If I knew that I wouldn't be sitting here," snapped Jason.

"So you want the court to believe that you didn't kill your wife yourself; you have no idea who would want to kill your wife; and that you believe a complete stranger just walked by, decided to slip in, grab a knife from the kitchen and commence to stabbing LeAnn 27 times for no reason at all. Is that your claim?" he asked as he paced back and forth in front of the jury.

"Yes! I didn't kill her, no one we know killed her, so it had to be someone we don't know!" he yelled.

The Prosecutor turns to the jury and looks directly at them before making his next statement. "Keep in mind that she was stabbed from behind 27 times. This means that not only did the killer know her, he couldn't look her in the eyes when he did it," he said watching Jason stir.

"If the cops would actually look then maybe they could find who actually did it instead of only focusing on me," he said frustrated.

"Are you referring to the same cops that actually did 'look' and found your duffle bag of athletic gear and shoes covered in LeAnn's blood? Those cops?" he asked looking at the jury with his eyebrows raised.

"That was stolen out of my car!" yelled Jason almost unable to sit still in his chair.

"Was it? I'm sorry I must have missed where you filed the police report," he said sarcastically.

"I didn't file one," Jason said looking furious.

"How was it stolen out of your car? Did they break a window; break into the trunk? Where was your bag exactly?" asked the Prosecutor walking closer to the stand taunting Jason.

"Look it was just gone okay! It was there in the morning, then gone when I got off work. I went for drinks and when I came home LeAnn was dead and they told me about the bag later. I didn't kill my wife!" yelled Jason.

"That's a very detailed account that you've given us Jason. Let me see if I can fill in any of the details for you though. You went for 'drinks' after work, which we established weeks ago was you going to one of your many mistresses lofts and having sex; you returned to find your wife upset that you've been cheating on her; you calmly quiet her and tell her how much you love her, maybe make her some tea, then you hand her that tea and commence to stabbing her to death from behind 27 times! And when you're finished, you simply wash off the knife, put it up, run down the alley and dump your bloody clothes, come back and change so that it looks like you came directly home from 'drinks'. Then before calling 911 it doesn't even cross your mind that a man that actually loves his wife and comes home to find her stabbed in the living room floor, would immediately run to her, hold her, and try and revive her," stated the Prosecutor as he clicks a picture onto the screen of Jason's clothes he was wearing when he was arrested.

"Not a speck of blood. I assume that's because with your other clothes being completely soaked you'd had enough for the evening right?" he said sarcastically as he pointed to the picture.

"This is bullshit!" yelled Jason standing up and yelling to the back of the Prosecutor that was already walking back to his table.

"No further questions your honor," said the Prosecutor smiling and taking his seat as he watched the expressions of shock and discontentment spread across the faces of the jury as they watched Jason walk back to the defense table.

The day of the verdict Calvin sat in the back of the courtroom in the corner where Jason wouldn't notice him. As the Judge asked Jason to rise for the verdict he laughed to himself loving the fact that he was such an insignificant human being to Jason that the thought of Calvin killing LeAnn had never once crossed Jason's mind. And that, was Calvin's specialty. He loved playing games and he loved winning. He couldn't contain his smile as he thought about his stats. He was currently undefeated.

"Has the jury reached a verdict?" asked the Judge.

"We have your Honor," said the Foreman.

"What say you?" he asked.

"In the charge of Murder in the First Degree, we find the Defendant, Guilty."

As Jason begins to break down from the verdict Calvin smiles and turns to exit saying quietly to himself, "Checkmate bitch."

Jasmine

Jasmine was snuggled in her bed dreaming that she was a white seagull just hanging in the air, enjoying the view of the ocean. The sun was beginning to rise on a new day.

"Senorita Jasmine! Senorita por favor!" yelled Lucinda their morning housekeeper trying to wake her.

Jasmine was trying to shake off the pill she had taken and wake up. The one thing that she graciously accepted from Henry was acting classes. She had made it a point to be in any drama related activity that she could. It had allowed her to escape from her own reality and to be a master of her emotions. It was time for her to cash in on those lessons.

"Que es la problema senora?" asked Jasmine sleepily.

"Tu madre senorita Jasmine, sigame por favor. Ahora por favor!" yelled Lucinda pulling the covers back to reveal Jasmine in her nightgown barefoot looking freshly wakened.

"Okay Lucinda I'm coming, I'm coming," said Jasmine groggy following behind her as if she had no idea what was happening.

As the two began crossing the main foyer the lights to police cars could be seen coming around the circle drive. Jasmine was smiling to herself loving the timing. Instead of putting on a show for Lucinda only she would get to have a crowd.

Jasmine turns with Lucinda on her arm and they walk to the front door opening it. Two female detectives are approaching cautiously keeping their hands next to their weapons as the door opens. There are several patrol cars that have blocked the entrance to the property and were maintaining the perimeter.

"What's going on?" asked Jasmine looking confused. To this point all she was supposed to know is that Lucinda is saying there's something wrong with her mother. She hadn't mentioned she had already called the police but Jasmine was glad that she had.

"Miss, I'm Detective Martinez, this is my partner Detective Carroll. We're responding to a call from the residence that there is a possible homicide...."

Before Martinez can continue Jasmine whirls around and starts running for her mother's room as if that was the first she had heard of it.

"Damn it," said Martinez under her breath. This is what she didn't want to happen but there's not many options when it comes to announcing why they were there.

Lucinda had started after Jasmine so Martinez and Carroll ran behind her. It seemed like they had went through a museum before finally reaching the back of the property to the master suite. Before they had made it through the main lounging area to the bedroom they could hear Jasmine begin screaming at the top of her lungs.

"No! Mom no! What the fuck! Mom you didn't!" screamed Jasmine as tears streamed down her face and she hysterically began shaking Priscilla as if to try and revive her. Jasmine continued screaming at her as she ran her hands over her face and her hair then just held onto her and cried. Priscilla's blood was all over her as she acted as though the thought of the woman in her arms dying would be the end of the world as she knew it. Ironically, it was just that.

Jasmine laid on a gurney in the back of the ambulance staring at Detective Martinez trying to focus on her face. Something about her face seemed familiar and made her feel peaceful.

"Look Jasmine I'm sorry we had to sedate you. I'm not even going to try to find something comforting to say because I know what you just had to see. We need to take you to the hospital to make sure you're okay. Physically, but more importantly, mentally. I know it's hard to lose a parent and then not be able to stay at home or with anything familiar, but it's necessary. I'll come see you this evening. If you think of something you want from your room make sure they let me know," said Martinez smiling at Jasmine and squeezing her hand.

"Thank you," said Jasmine as a tear streamed down her face. She didn't know how to handle the mixture of emotions she was being overwhelmed with so she simply squeezed her hand back, then closed her eyes and laid her head back feeling the tracks of hot tears make their way down her cheeks.

—∘∘∢●⊱∘∘—

Martinez walks back to the bedroom saying a prayer for Jasmine. It had been a long time since she had seen pain like that on another person's face and she was deeply moved by Jasmine.

Walking into the bedroom Carroll is gloved and holding a letter that is covered in blood but still legible in most places. She has a serious look on her face that Martinez has seen before.

"Call ahead of her and tell them to pull a rape kit," said Carroll handing the letter to Martinez.

Pulling gloves from her belt pouch Martinez felt her heart drop as she put them on then took the letter and read it. After finishing it she walked over to Henry's side of the bed and looked at his face.

"You got lucky that she just shot you in the back of your head you sorry bastard. I would have cut your dick off, shoved it down your fucking throat, then duck taped your mouth shut enjoying every minute it took for you to die," said Martinez wanting to spit in his face.

Carroll was looking closely at Priscilla making note of everything around her as well. "Why do you think mom offed herself?" she asked.

"How would you feel if your baby girl told you that your husband had been touching her for the past two years right in front of you and you didn't know it?" asked Martinez.

"I'd feel pretty fucked up no doubt. I have to say it looks like her dinner consisted of snacks, two bottles of wine and two bottles of pills. I'm surprised she could read or do anything," said Carroll looking to see how many pills were left in each bottle.

"The people that live on this hill sweat Prozac and fine wine. What're you talking about," smirked Martinez.

Carroll can't help but smile at her knowing that she was right.

Martinez looks through the glass at Jasmine laying in the bed looking out the window. She didn't know why she felt drawn to Jasmine, but she was. It wasn't in her nature to attach herself to anyone but she knew that Jasmine had no family and no real friends or anyone she could count on. She would be turning 18 in two days and would be alone.

Martinez knocked on the glass and waved at Jasmine as she looked at her. Then entered as Jasmine motioned for her to come inside.

She walked over to the chair beside of Jasmine's bed and sat down smiling at her. Jasmine smiled back looking better than the last time she had seen her.

"I know this is a shitty question but how are you?" she asked truly wondering how Jasmine was feeling.

"I'm fine thank you. It just doesn't seem real I guess. I'm used to going days, even weeks without seeing or speaking to her sometimes. That stupid fortress was so huge we could all be home for days and still not see each other," Jasmine said smiling.

"Has the social worker been in to talk to you yet?" asked Martinez.

"Yes. She said that since I'm about to turn 18 then there's no need to place me anywhere. I can just stay where I please," she said trying not to seem too happy.

"And where will you be staying?" Martinez asked.

"Henry's attorneys have already been in to see me. I've already signed to receive a loft and 5 million in exchange for not releasing to the media details about his 'indiscretions'," she said smiling.

"Are you okay with that? I can get someone to represent you if you need me to," said Martinez concerned.

"Honestly I can't go through it. It may sound shallow, or weak, or whatever, but I just want to start over. And I do have to say that I hated Henry but being poor sucks. If I have to live my life by myself at least

I can live it not on the streets and not having to rehash every detail of the last two years," Jasmine looked at Martinez in the eyes as this was a true statement that she needed to hang onto with dear life.

"I understand Jasmine. 5 million is a lot of money. I've seen where you lived for the last two years but something tells me you're not the diamonds and gold kind of girl. If you ever want to slum it in the real world call me anytime. I'd be happy to settle for hot dogs and a walk around the park for you to update me on how you're doing. I'm not sure where you're going to go or what you're going to do but I do want to tell you that I hope you find out who you are Jasmine. I hope that you find peace in yourself," said Martinez smiling at her.

"I hope I find that too. It's been eluding me for a very long time," said Jasmine as a small smile played at her lips.

Jasmine stood on the balcony of her loft looking over across the lights to the ocean beyond. She smiled and took in a deep breath. Walking back inside, she clicked on the news and ran with the excitement of a little kid to the couch in front of the TV. On the coffee table in front of her was a birthday cake that had an 18 on it with a fork on the left and to the right was a birthday cocktail she had made to toast herself. As the news came on Jasmine grabbed her glass and listened to the broadcast.

"The recent deaths at the Smith Mansion have now officially been ruled a Murder/Suicide. It's been reported that the daughter of Mrs. Smith had disclosed abuse from Henry Smith to her through a letter. That letter was found at the scene and police believe is the motivation for Pricilla Smith fatally shooting her multi-million dollar husband and then turning the gun on herself," stated the news anchor.

Jasmine smiled then lifted her glass to the TV in a toast.

"Happy Birthday to me."

The End